PROJECT
HUMAN PHASE
BOOK SIX

MW00529238

JS MORIN

HUMAN PHASE

PROJECT TRANSHUMAN: BOOK SIX

J.S. MORIN

Copyright © 2017 J.S. Morin

All rights reserved. No part of this publication may be reproduced, distributed or transmitted in any form or by any means, including photocopying, recording, or other electronic or mechanical methods, without the prior written permission of the publisher, except in the case of brief quotations embodied in critical reviews and certain other noncommercial uses permitted by copyright law. For permission requests, write to the publisher, addressed "Attention: Permissions Coordinator," at the address below.

Magical Scrivener Press
8941 Atlanta Ave, #280
Huntington Beach, CA 92646

www.magicalscrivener.com

Publisher's Note: This is a work of fiction. Names, characters, places, and incidents are a product of the author's imagination. Locales and public names are sometimes used for atmospheric purposes. Any resemblance to actual people, living or dead, or to businesses, companies, events, institutions, or locales is completely coincidental.

Ordering Information: Special discounts are available on quantity purchases by corporations, associations, and others. For details, contact the publisher at the address above.

J.S. Morin — First Edition

ISBN: 978-1-942642-72-5

Printed in the United States of America

CHAPTER ONE

Kaylee Fourteen wiped sweat from her forehead as she checked and rechecked the alignment of Mars' first locally built atmosphere generator. The turbine would be spinning at half a million revolutions per minute once activated, and the slightest misalignment of the meter-long blades could cause them to shatter against the casing at supersonic speeds. Her breath echoed from inside the mask of her portable oxygen supply, working on the exterior of the machine. Baking red sunlight filtered through the thick miasma of carbon dioxide, nitrogen, and methane that sustained the planet's first outdoor plant life. Soon—possibly within the decade—Kaylee would be able to picnic with her family under that sky without special equipment.

Tucking the nanoscale scanner into its holster on her belt, Kaylee tapped at the corner of her data goggles. She scrolled through her contacts list and connected to Ned Lund, the project lead for the Mars Terraforming Initiative and Kaylee's boss. "All set, Ned. We can cap the outlet nozzle on atmo pump one. All seventy-two blades check out. All fittings exact within the micron. Thermal expansion zone is clear."

Ned's gruff voice came back in her ear. "Throw a tarp over it. We'll cap pump one after lunch."

Kaylee secured the site. Magnetic tie-downs clamped the pale purple alienite tarp across the exposed opening of the turbine. The last thing any of them needed was to come back from lunch break to find a grain of sand carried on the wind and dinged one of the blades. A quick double-check that the tarp wasn't going to move while she was gone, Kaylee maneuvered the bucket of her lift-arm truck to deposit her at ground level.

Hopping the safety chain that kept her from falling out, Kaylee hustled over to one of the group transports and squeezed in beside a coworker on a bench in the back. The ride to base camp was only five minutes. Walking would have taken nearly an hour. Being jammed in shoulder-to-shoulder with people she barely knew was worth the time savings.

Once back at the pre-fab collection of environmentally controlled structures, Kaylee waited in line and made her way through the airlock in the third batch of workers. Once inside the cafeteria, she pushed her goggles onto her scalp and unbuckled her oxygen mask. The first breath of free-floating air always tasted better than the dank, rubbery-smelling stuff from inside the mask. Kaylee filled her lungs, and the sheen of sweat around her nose and mouth cooled and dried.

"Good work out there, Fourteen," Ned greeted her with a handshake. His palm was callused and rough; his grip like iron. "We might get that unit online by nightfall at this rate."

Kaylee stifled a yawn. "I thought we might push through lunch..."

Ned shook his head as he picked up a tray and got in line for chow. "Right is better than fast. That's half the reason you're here. Adrian wanted fast, but he got sloppy. We're not robots. Food. Rest. The body works best when you maintain it."

Kaylee fought back another yawn as she retrieved a tray and perused the camp's lunch fare. All of it was Earth-grown, shipped across seventy-nine million kilometers of orbital space, and manufactured to last. Inside the colonies, more and more local food was consumed, but out in the work camps, they ate the cheap stuff.

"Sorry, Ned," Kaylee said. "Don't mean to seem like I'm—"

Ned waved a hand, brushing her apology aside. "Nah. Takes getting used to. Forty minutes a day doesn't sound like much, but those short Earth days you're used to will take their toll. Happens to everyone their first couple months here."

Kaylee smiled her reply as the two of them piled their trays with canned peaches, beef jerky in gravy, and vacuum-packed broccoli. They'd all been so nice since she arrived. Everyone back home had warned her about the Martians and their bias against Earthborn humans, but Kaylee had yet to experience that bias firsthand.

She joined Ned and a few of the other supervisor-level workers at one of the main tables. Kaylee was Quality Assurance Chief, a role that had seemed to elude the Martians despite their attempts to fill it from their own ranks. Around the table were Chief Logistics Officer Miriam Hazra, Chief Technical Officer Ben Santos, and Operations

Manager Lijing Chang. They all scooted and rearranged their trays to make room for the two newcomers at the round, plastic table.

"Heard we might cap the nozzle this afternoon," Lijing said, raising a paltry toast with her thermos of water.

"To Kaylee," Ned said, playing along and raising his thermos as well. The others followed suit. "May our next turbine activation not blow up in our faces like the last one."

"Hear, hear," the others joined in, including a halfhearted Kaylee. Stainless steel bottles clanged. Everyone chuckled, then dug into their meals.

No one was overly formal on the project. They were all sitting around a Protofab-grade table with environmental hazard gear dangling loose from their clothing. All of them were sweaty and dirty with a powdery red coating of untamed soil from outside the dome. Perfunctory discussions of work-related topics soon gave way to chatting about the latest movies, soccer, and the upcoming Emancipation Day celebration on Earth.

When talk crept toward politics, Kaylee wolfed down the last of her soggy, vacuum-preserved broccoli, and excused herself. "Time to prep that turbine for low-speed testing."

The rest of them gave a quick acknowledgment and returned to discussing local elections.

Kaylee pulled down her goggles, fixed her filtration mask back in place, and stepped out into the dusty Martian wilderness. She took a breath in the privacy of her own company, and the rubbery smell came as a welcome reprise.

CHAPTER TWO

Eve Fourteen sat on the edge of a pristine white table covered in bed linens. To call the piece of medical equipment a bed would have given it too much credit for an intention toward comfort, rest, or peace of mind. She wore a white smock provided by the hospital and was covered in residue from a variety of lubricants, adhesives, and conductive solutions that had been part of her physical examination.

Doctors had an annoying propensity for thoroughness, and with Eve they were particularly mindful. After all, at 148 years old, the pillar of human society's health wasn't a subject to be taken lightly.

Ashley390 returned. Despite the changing fashions of the time, the old robot still wore a chassis that had a distinctly inhuman appearance with an exposed metalized plastic finish and glowing orange eyes. Eve found the latter comforting, even though not many of her younger colleagues agreed.

"Would you like this as a summary or a list of defects?" the doctor asked.

Eve smiled weakly. It was her own fault for insisting they not sugarcoat anything. "You've had me here five hours already. I think I have time for both."

Ashley390 referenced a datatab despite having access to all the information she needed internally. Eve allowed the affectation to pass without remark. "You are the healthiest 148-year-old woman on record. That said, you're still the only one, and in broader terms, I think you ought to strongly consider retirement and spending more time with your family."

Eve snorted and crossed her thin, frail arms. "Humanity *is* my family. And the second that someone convinces me they can do my job better, I'll let them have it."

Ashley390 shook her head in resignation and continued. "Your renal function is continuing to slip. I think it's about time we replace the other one with—"

"Fine," Eve said with a wave of her hand. "Another cybernetic part. I don't have a particular attachment to a kidney."

"Your lungs are still a trouble spot, but I know you've been hesitant to have them upgraded."

"Lot of bother," Eve muttered. "The recovery time is too long. Get it under three days, and I'll consider it."

"You're not going to like this next item," Ashley390 warned. "But..."

"Oh, spit it out, woman," Eve snapped. "You tell me I've not got long to live; well, don't waste time coddling my feelings. Bad news has yet to get better with keeping, and I daresay I've heard worse than what you're going to say next."

"You need a crystalline brain."

"The hell I do," Eve countered, slipping gingerly off the table to face Ashley390 directly. "You've been pushing a robotic brain on me for years. I haven't changed my mind, and I surely haven't changed my vote on Human Welfare Committee policy regarding human upload in either direction."

Not backing down a millimeter, Ashley390 set her datatab aside and spread her hands. "That's me not 'coddling your feelings,'" she quoted Eve's words in a digital mimicry of the elder human's voice. "Despite our best efforts to keep it at bay, you're developing neural plaque that will eventually cause irreversible loss of higher brain function."

Eve rolled her bionic implant eyes, which still saw as clearly as a teenager's. "Spare me the theatrics. Up the dose on those cleansing microbes you've been using, and send me on my way."

"Any more aggressive treatment is just going to exacerbate another issue. The anti-amyloid bacteria produce waste chemicals that are beginning to cause issues of their own. We don't have the time to develop and test countermeasures that would be safe to use within your lifetime."

Eve snorted. "I've been accused of spouting excrement often enough. About time I had justification for its origins."

Ashley390's smile was a sad one. "Geriatrics is a new old science. You're in uncharted territory, Eve. You get the cutting edge of every procedure we come up with. We're two decades past the oldest patients the Human Era ever documented. Left to its own biological limitations, that cellular brain of yours might have anywhere from three to eighteen months left of useful life in it."

"After that?" Eve asked. Let Ashley390 try to scare her. Let the robot lay out all the bleak prognoses she liked. See if that might change Eve's mind.

It wouldn't. But Eve still had to know her fate.

Ashley390 affected a sigh. "Disorientation. Irritability. Memory and cognitive degeneration. We can regulate all your involuntary functions mechanically, but you'd essentially be a cybernetic puppet with limp strings."

"How cheery," Eve said, shuffling to the corner of the examination room to retrieve her clothing. "Anything else I need to know about my imminent demise?"

"I know you've got a busy schedule the next few days," Ashley390 said. "But we should probably swap out your bronchial filter and replace a few more of your afferent nerves."

An alert popped up in Eve's field of vision.

INCOMING TRANSMISSION.

"Pardon me," Eve said with a raised hand to stem further prognoses from the doctor. "Work intrudes. They must be losing bladder control over me being gone this long."

"Not everyone's bladder has a servo-controlled regulator valve," Ashley390 commented.

Eve's fingers twitched. Fiber strands carried neuromuscular signals to the computer interface that had become as much a part of her as any organ. She navigated the interface to bounce messages back and forth across the Solarwide with her secretaries and a junior member of the Human Welfare Committee. In between, she creaked and groaned her way into a pair of slacks, an auto-button blouse, and orthotic shoes.

"Any last admonishments?" Eve asked as she headed for the door amid the floodgate she'd opened to committee business.

"All I can do is advise and offer treatment options," Ashley390 replied. "I've made my recommendations. I can't make you heed them."

Eve smiled from the doorway. "Wonderful system, isn't it? I'm free to live the last of my life on my terms, not yours."

CHAPTER THREE

Kaylee arrived at home that evening, worn to the bone but with a weary smile on her face. Her husband, Alan, greeted her at the door with a hug despite her being caked with crud from the day's work.

"How'd it go? Are we breathing life into Mars yet?" Alan asked. He wore his sweater and tie like a uniform along with a sappy, optimistic smile that went with everything. He hadn't changed since getting back from school that afternoon, where he taught history and sociology.

Kaylee hung from his neck for support. "Finally. You know, I said I wanted to come to Mars to make a difference, work with my hands, get out of my cushy climate projection job and away from computer terminals."

"Reconsidering? I can have our bags packed inside the hour," Alan joked.

Kaylee stretched and headed for the kitchen. She opened the refrigerator and pulled out a bottle of locally produced orange juice. "Not on your life. Today I got to see a jet of supersonic gas inject our atmosphere with the first breathable air made by Martians."

"Are we calling ourselves Martians now?" Alan asked as he set out a pair of champagne glasses for Kaylee to fill.

Kaylee scrunched her face into a thoughtful scowl. "I suppose I did call it 'our' atmosphere, didn't I? Well, it's mine, at least. I helped make it, even if I didn't build or install any of the machinery. It was my sign-off that allowed Ned to flip the switch and turn it on."

"Like a priestess blessing her new flock," Alan said with a smirk. He lifted his orange juice in a toast.

Kaylee clinked her glass against Alan's. "To being Martians."

They drank their toast, refilled their glasses, and sat down with auto-cooked fettuccine alfredo in front of the video screen. Alan flipped on the news feeds.

It was a daily ritual. The Solarwide brought Earth in story-item doses that vaccinated them against homesickness. Much as she might claim to have embraced her new Martian home, Kaylee still clung to that ball of ocean-drenched rock where she'd been born.

"In sporting news, the—"

Alan tapped the remote, switching from the London feed to Philadelphia-2.

"...and elsewhere in the solar system, the Mars—"

Tap.

"Wait," Kaylee said, grabbing Alan by the wrist and knocking her fork to the floor with a clatter. "Go back. That was our atmosphere generator."

Normally, the last thing they were looking for on the news feeds was Earth's take on Martian current events, but this was an exception. Alan flicked back and resumed Philadelphia-2's coverage, backing it up to the point they'd left off.

"The Mars Terraforming Initiative activated its first homegrown atmosphere generator, a new design that promises to create a breathable biome by 3225."

"Technically," Kaylee said as an aside to the broadcast. "The plants will do most of the work. We're nudging the system toward a critical mass of self-sufficiency."

Alan pointed at the screen. "Hey, isn't that your boss?"

Kaylee nodded, scowling at the sight of Ned giving an interview in the shadow of the generator. He had his breather off. Portable spigots, tapped off the main line, were washing an area around Ned and the reporter with breathable air.

Showoff.

"I know this is a proud day for Mars," Ned said from the screen. By the waning daylight, the interview must have been recorded less than an hour ago. *"This baby and all its subsystems run on a single Truman-Effect reactor. They've got another ready for us at Site-2. This was just the first of many atmo generators. Still have plenty of work to do. But we're Martians. We'll roll up our sleeves and get this done our way, without any help from Earth."*

Alan and Kaylee shared a glance. Where would Ned's team have been without Kaylee overseeing the quality of the installation? And what planet did they think they'd gotten her from? Venus?

"*Why is it so important that this effort was entirely human-run?*" the reporter asked. "*Terraforming Committee estimates show that this project could have been completed in 3215 with a robotic workforce.*"

"I tell you what, Kent," Ned said. "*If those robots had wanted Mars habitable, they damn well could have done it centuries ago. They had their chance, and sure, maybe they could've done it quicker. But Martians—hell, all humans—need to look after themselves and not wait for committee handouts to do everything for them. That's why this is so important. This is the beginning of a free, self-sufficient Mars.*"

Alan blinked. "Did he just say that over the Solarwide?"

"He did," Kaylee confirmed, hardly believing it herself.

It was one thing talking politics in the cafeteria of a small, close-knit project team. Plenty of Martians grumbled about being second-class citizens on their own planet. But to publicly come out *against* robots?

"How can you work for someone so backward-thinking?" Alan asked. "I don't know if I could put up with it."

The news feed continued on. "*Elsewhere on Mars, protesters disrupted an Agriculture Committee tour of the Curiosity orchards—*"

Tap.

"It's getting worse by the day," Alan said softly. "I mean, it's still a minority. It's still just rabble-rousers. But I hear the stuff kids are picking up at home, the ideas their parents leave lying around like charged blasters. I hope I get through to them, but I worry how many internalize those messages."

Kaylee looked at him askew. "Why haven't you said anything? You always seem so upbeat when you get home."

"When *you* get home," Alan countered. "By then I've had time to unwind. And don't get me wrong; the kids are great. It's just that... once in a while..."

"Speaking of kids," Kaylee said. "Wonder if ours are still awake."

Alan performed a quick swipe on the remote control, and the video screen displayed dual clocks for the cities of Curiosity and Oxford. "It's 10:15 there. They'll have been in bed a while by now."

"But..." Kaylee started to object. Then her shoulders fell. "I hate that forty minutes we gain here every day. Or lose. However you want to look at it. It's like Athena and Stephen are drifting away in time as well as orbital space."

"Hey. It's Emancipation Day tomorrow," Alan said in a weak effort to cheer her up. "In four or five years, it'll be Athena's turn. Another couple for Stephen. Maybe they'll decide to come live on Mars."

Kaylee's gaze strayed to the darkened window of their apartment. The domed city of Curiosity lay beyond the opaque smartglass. Their first few weeks on Mars, they'd kept it clear, soaking in the novelty. Now, they rarely let the outside view in with them. "I'm not sure whether I'll want them here five years from now. Not the way things are heading."

CHAPTER FOUR

E ve stood at a lectern overlooking a crowd of fifty-five fresh young faces. They were children and would remain so even after this day. Legally speaking, they would be emancipated, of course, but 130 years separated Eve from even the eldest among them. There were men and women with gray hair and stooped backs whom Eve still considered children. Her children. Every last one of them.

It was a vain conceit. Eve had never borne a single child. She had never experienced firsthand the pain of childbirth, the hormonal rush of holding a newborn after carrying it within her for nine months. But she had been a mother. She and Plato had raised one daughter together. As head of the Human Welfare Committee, Eve had played nursemaid to all the rest. Oh, there were a few near her own age to whom she had been more a sister, a cousin, or an aunt, but this wasn't a day to quibble over exceptions.

Eve gripped the lectern in both hands. She tried to tell herself that it was to appear dramatic, forceful, and in command. She was there to inspire them, not remind them that standing for twenty minutes at a stretch was a terrible strain on her old muscles.

"Welcome, friends and family. Welcome, dignitaries, officials, and media. But most of all, welcome, Emancipation Class of 3217. As I look out upon you, I see the future. No, not as a prophet but as a visionary. You are the writers of the future yet unwritten. Humanity is a river. Each year at this time, we add new tributaries to that river. Each year, that river grows larger, wider, deeper, grander. You are a part of that. The choices you make from this day forward will shape humanity in large ways and small, by intention and by accident, by word and by deed.

"Most of you have already decided upon a career. Six of you have chosen to go into the field of robotics. Eight intend to study genetics. Two are set for solar exploration. Eleven of you will be moving to the Mars colony. Two pairs of you will be heading straight from this ceremony to the Madagascar Center for Human Advancement to have your DNA sampled for parenthood. I will not single out anyone today, nor will I delve into each and every professional commitment made by this gathering. I draw attention to those whose decisions have already been made in order to contrast with the more interesting among you — the undecided.

"Freedom. Choice. Imagination. Do not despair, those among you whose path in life has not been cut clear ahead of you. The greatest journeys begin with no destination in sight. When I was your age, I could never have conceived of the life ahead of me. The position I hold, the home I live in, the very species to which we all belong, none of it existed as we know it today. There was no Human Welfare Committee. The only homes were for robots. Humanity was a mere science experiment aimed at reviving a distant past. Think on this: what does not exist today that you will bring into existence within your lifetime?"

Eve scanned the crowd for reactions. She didn't care about the parents and hangers on. It was the eyes of the newly emancipated that interested her. Bright, eager, intelligent, they watched her as they processed the words of her speech. There was greatness out there. Where, she could not say. Not all promise is fulfilled. The deepest depths of potential are rarely plumbed. Was her successor out there? Was the next Prime Minister in the crowd? The next da Vinci? The next Truman? Was there something beyond all of them that Eve couldn't conceive of yet?

She hoped so.

Eve's greatest wish was for humanity to leave her in its wake.

"And so it is with a —" a fit of coughing choked off Eve's words. After a brief pause, she composed herself. "It is with a glad heart and joyous spirit that —"

Eve tried to suck in a breath that wouldn't come. The speech had taken too much out of her, straining ancient lungs that Ashley390 kept insisting she replace. Clutching the lectern for support, Eve tried to remain upright. The world wobbled. Horrified gasps escaped the crowd.

What have they got to be upset about? They're not the ones dying.

Warnings and error messages flashed across Eve's vision. She didn't need to be told that her oxygen-intake level was unacceptably low, that her heart rate had spiked, or that she was in need of medical attention. Notification that she had already sent an emergency medical beacon was welcome but unnecessary.

Mere seconds passed before medical help arrived. The nannies and worrywarts among robotkind and humanity alike forebade Eve going anywhere without a doctor practically within arm's reach.

Eve passed out surrounded by the finest medical minds on Earth.

CHAPTER FIVE

N ed Lund slipped through the door of his apartment with a grunt of relief. Yapping with that reporter from Philadelphia-2 had squeezed the last of the juice out of him, but it had been worth it. Those crystal-brained number crunchers back on Earth needed to know that Mars was up here taking care of business for itself.

"Darla?" Ned bellowed. There could have been no mistaking the sound of his arrival. The door was in need of repair and opened and closed with a gravelly chatter.

"Back here," his wife's melodious voice floated from her home office. Just hearing it brightened Ned's mood. "I'm almost finished updating this mineral profile."

Ned lumbered across the living room and collapsed onto the couch. "No hurry. Kids home yet?"

"Been and gone," Darla called back. "Abel's off to debate club, and Melissa's got soccer practice."

Ned nodded. Poor kids. He owed them better than to work such late hours. It had been easier when Horace had been project lead, but Horace had to go and get himself elected to the colonial council.

"You had dinner yet?"

"I fed the kids, but I waited for you."

"In or out?"

"Oh, in," Darla assured him. "I won't drag you through a shower and out into public again. Just let me finish this up and I'll program the food processor. Any special requests to mark a momentous occasion?"

Ned smiled a weary, satisfied smile. He'd lived in Darla's shadow so long getting treated like someone famous was taking used to. She was Mars' leading hydroponics researcher. Martians appreciated someone whose whole career revolved around feeding them without Earth's handouts. But now Ned wasn't just an assistant operations supervisor; he was project lead. That was practically equal footing. "You see me on Philadelphia-2?"

"You know I can't watch you on news feeds. And I object to those biased Earth-centric feeds on principle. I don't want my media metrics showing support for Earth broadcasts. What if I run for office next year?"

"Right. Yeah. Dumb to ask. Sorry."

Darla entered the living room, dressed for a casual day or remote login programming in pajamas and slippers. She had her data goggles pushed up onto her head. "Don't be like that. Let *me* cook for *you* tonight. You've earned it."

Ned gave a weak smile that turned genuine after Darla leaned down for a welcome-home kiss. "Steak. Recon. With El Paso sauce."

Darla chuckled. Ned could imagine the roll of her eyes without needing to look toward the kitchen. "I know it's local, but reconstituted proteins *aren't* steak no matter what shape you program it."

"Maybe when we have an atmosphere, we'll have space for herds of our own. For now, I want a steak some robot didn't feed."

As Darla busied herself with a meal-programming task that might take upward of two minutes, Ned closed his eyes and tried to see if he could get every muscle in his body to relax at once. But as soon as he came close to achieving his goal of perfect relaxation, a chime from his pocket startled him.

Digging out his portable, Ned saw that it was Miriam. He was within his rights to blow off the call—she worked for him after all, not the other way around. But if his Chief Logistics Officer was calling after hours, it had to be something urgent. "What? I'm about to have a home-cooked meal."

"Have you seen the news feeds?" Miriam blurted.

"I was just on 'em."

"Not that," Miriam snapped. "But good. I wanted you to hear it from me. Our dark matter order has been hijacked. Reactor 2 is going to be delayed by six weeks."

"What?" Ned demanded, clutching the portable computer hard enough that he worried about breaking it. "Hijacked? By who?"

"Kanto," Miriam spat bitterly. "Who else. Jason90 has a miniaturized Truman-Effect reactor that he's planning on installing in a new chassis. He pulled some backdoor committee maneuver and got our shipment diverted."

Ned threw the portable across the room. Miriam gave a startled yelp at the loud crack when it hit the wall. "Ned... you still there?" Miriam's tiny voice crackled from the portable.

Stalking over to retrieve the undamaged computer—which he now felt foolish for thinking he could damage with his grip—Ned scooped it back up. "'Course I am," he snapped. "Now tell me what I'm supposed to do with a crew of twenty-five and no reactor?"

"We could still start—"

"Don't even try that," Ned bellowed into the portable. "Without an on-site reactor, we won't be able to power half our equipment. We'll be running relays back to Curiosity for battery recharges. That's no way to run a terraforming team. How about explaining how you let this happen. Aren't you *on* the Resource Allocation Committee?"

"As an observer," Miriam replied. "No vote, remember? Anyway, with Jason90 putting his weight behind it, it wouldn't have mattered if I had a vote or not. All those robotic committee members could see themselves with Truman-Effect Reactors in their next upgrade and couldn't vote for it fast enough. To hell with Mars."

Ned remained silent. Lost in thought. There were tasks he could have the project team shift onto—minor, nitpicking necessities, none of which struck him as urgent. Site surveys and equipment overhauls didn't make the news feeds, but someone had to do them. Problem was, Ned was staffed for generator installation. He'd be farming out his techs to the biological reconditioning teams just to keep them all busy.

"Ned...? You got a plan?"

He felt his gorge rising. An hour ago, he'd been on top of the solar system. Now, he was scrounging for table scraps beneath the robots' feast.

Again.

For now, though, he had to tell Miriam something. "Maybe we can see about getting a temporary fusion reactor approved for Site 2."

"Fusion?" Miriam asked incredulously. "You *know* any nuclear tech is banned Mars-wide."

"Hence the approval," Ned reasoned. "Byproduct will be letting everyone know just how bad we needed that dark matter. Heck, I don't even *want* the fusion reactor. I want to light a fire under the slow-moving clods at Opportunity to get them to do something about the Resource Allocation Committee."

"On it, boss," Miriam replied.

The call ended.

"Did the other half of that conversation sound as bad as your end?" Darla asked, poking her head in from the kitchen amid the wafting scent of grilled steak.

"Nah," Ned said. "Nothing I can't handle."

CHAPTER SIX

Alan clung to Kaylee's arm as they entered the back offices of the First Martian Theater. The young woman holding the door gave the couple a tight, reassuring smile hinting that she understood their trepidation. The décor was all new, with plasticized steel walls molded to look like old stonework and red velvet drapes from a top-end cloth-o-matic piled in rolled bundles ready to be installed as a stage curtain. Their escort led them down a brightly lit corridor that still managed to feel foreboding despite the smell of fresh paint.

They passed through an old-fashioned swinging door labeled "cast break room" and found themselves attending a gathering that looked halfway between a poker game and the cliché Human Era cartoons of cigar-smoking old men who ran corrupt political campaigns.

A thin-faced man with a welcoming smile beckoned them over. "Kaylee, Alan, glad you could make it. Mars is always in need of citizens looking to help their community. Sit down. Let me introduce everyone."

Kaylee separated herself from her husband and shook hands with Bob Volkov, Nancy Davis, Abel McCovey, Candice Medina, and Annabel Santos, plus Andy Wilkes, their host. She tried to remember all the names, but she'd always been better with numbers than faces. Alan was the people person, meeting the same neighbors with the same handshakes and likely having permanently associated all those new names with their owners already. For him, they were just another class of students to learn.

"You probably have a lot of questions," Andy said as Kaylee and Alan joined the group around the table. "We're willing to answer any you might have."

"Is all this...committee-approved?" Alan asked, glancing nervously around the room as if to check for hidden cameras or microphones.

Andy chuckled at perfect ease. "Tacitly. Most of the robots know *something* is going on over here, and they don't want to get involved. They like it that way. Mars is their little pet porcupine. They like having us, but every time they get too close they end up regretting it. The Colonist Fitness Screenings, regulation of Truman-Effect technology, local schooling certification, independent emancipation boards; every time they try to help, the worse they make things. I think they're banking their drone credits on the Unity Keepers holding Mars together."

Unity Keepers. It sounded so stuffy and formal, like a Solar Age reincarnation of the Knights Templar or a twentieth century cult. If their referral hadn't come from one of Alan's teaching colleagues, Kaylee might have walked out then and there.

But how sinister could an organization be if a kindergarten teacher was their leading recruiter?

"That's why we're here," Kaylee said. "It's the nightly news feeds. Our kids are still in school on Earth, and we watch the terrestrial news rather than embarrass them every night with a comm. But Mars is our home now, and night after night the stories get worse. Alan and I talked about it, and we realized we were waiting for someone to do something about it. We wanted the news feeds to come on one night with President Francoeur dusting his hands and telling us that the separatists and instigators had all been set straight, that everything was fine."

Alan leaned forward. "We realized we needed to be part of the solution."

Andy smiled patronizingly. "There's no solution here. We have no end game. The Mars First Party, the Humans First Party, the private Solarwide channels where secessionists and anti-mechanical bigots gather... none of that is going away in our lifetimes. We just push back, hinder, keep them from spreading. Education helps, but they've cut off Martian education from the Oxford curriculum now."

That had been a key factor in leaving Athena and Stephen at school on Earth. Whatever anyone said about robots, Nora109 had kept the standards at Oxford consistently excellent since it opened. The same couldn't be said of the Martian Colonial School System. The organization had seen eight different chief administrators during its seventeen years of operation and eight different curriculum standards. No chief administrator had yet to win reelection.

"We just want to do the right thing," Kaylee said. Alan nodded in agreement.

Andy shook his head. "I don't peddle easy answers here. That's for the other guys. But I can tell you this much. History doesn't look kindly on extremist groups, nor does it look kindly on colonial subjugation by distant governments."

Kaylee furrowed her brow. "But..."

Alan snickered. History was his forte. "You're saying that whosever viewpoint prevails writes the history."

"The Unity Keepers are offering a particularly tricky bit of history to write. It comes rife with villains who have families to worry about, jobs to safeguard, and self-esteem to shelter. We've got a rough outline to work from, but I'm mainly offering the two of you a blank text field to fill in. This isn't for everyone."

Feeling small in her chair, Kaylee nodded. Maybe they'd made a mistake coming here. Andy Wilkes was no visionary, no charismatic leader. He was just the director of a local theater group that didn't even perform original plays. Everything they did was a retread from Earth, from *Hamlet* to *Rent* to *First Girl on Earth*. Even the politics were recycled, it seemed.

Kaylee leaned forward to push her chair back. "Thank you for—"

Alan reached across the table in unison with Kaylee's lean. "For the opportunity. We're committed to making Mars a place where we can build a home for ourselves."

Kaylee hesitated. They'd often spoken about settling on Mars permanently, maybe having one or two more children once they'd gotten used to the relocation—Martian, born and raised. Their son, Stephen, had a different career in mind every time Kaylee asked, but every one of them involved space. His sister, Athena, was already talking internships at Kanto—no thoughts of Mars on that one's mind. Kaylee knew, deep down, that her kids were going to build their own lives, not follow her and Alan around the solar system.

Never fully formed, Kaylee's thoughts passed in a mushy blur of emotional footprints left by months of conversations with her husband. She found herself shaking Andy's hand in turn. "Mars *is* our home now. We're willing to do what it takes to keep the partnership with Earth intact."

CHAPTER SEVEN

The Solar Mining Committee met in the conference room of the West Virginia Orbital Ore Refinery. Ever since Jason12's self-termination 875 years ago, Jason90 had been in charge of production at Kanto. As the years rolled past, he found fewer and fewer reasons to leave the kingdom-sized factory. Each year, production demands rose. Each year, new designs and upgrades poured in from hobbyist inventors and his own crack team of roboticists. The demands on Jason90's time grew to fill in the gaps that had once held time for leisure.

This meeting was reason enough for Jason90 to make the trek to the far side of Earth to attend in person.

Projected on the planetarium-styled full-ceiling display was the scheduled mining operations for the upcoming three months. Scalable to show the entire Kuiper Belt or a single mining vessel, the screen could display travel routes, planetary and lunar orbits, ore collection rates and compositions, and IDs for every ship under committee purview.

Mining Committee chairman Jason266 shifted the planetarium view to focus on a mining transport on its return trip to the core of the solar system. "Vessel 87 is currently scheduled to make a stopover at Mars to deliver twenty kilotons of iron ore to the Curiosity colony before continuing onward to Kanto with the remainder of the load. However, we have an emergency request from the Directory of Production at Kanto. Jason90...?"

Jason90 stood and addressed his colleagues on the Solar Mining Committee. "As you are all aware, with the recent breakthrough in Truman-Effect technology, we are ramping up production of miniaturized reactors. The Version 85.0 is going to be in demand unlike any chassis design we've ever seen. We're currently averaging five power-supply rescues per year. There's even poor Toby79 on board that mining vessel, hooked up to ship's power on a tether because they ran out of working power cells. The theoretical mean time between failures on a chassis-compatible Truman-Effect Reactor is 625 years."

There were grumbles around the room. Jason90 increased his auditory gain until he could eavesdrop on all the conversations throughout the meeting hall. He heard complaints about chassis wait times getting longer, about personal troubles with existing power cells and recharge times, about the dependence on external power being a constant thorn in the back of a robot's mind that they weren't biological creatures.

It was easy to overlook that last point most of the time.

All of it was music to Jason90's ears. All but one voice, and that voice didn't require eavesdropping to be heard.

"How can you even consider this?" Miriam Hazra demanded, marching from her seat in the advisory members' section and storming over to the table reserved for voting members of the committee. "Mars needs that ore. You've already diverted our dark matter to Kanto. Now our only ore delivery this month?"

Jason266 spoke up, despite Miriam's ire being aimed squarely at Jason90. "Your position is duly noted, Ms. Hazra. I should like to point out that Mars has ample local sources of iron ore. Per the Martian Resource Extraction Committee's mandates, those reserves aren't eligible for shipment off world. Kanto is dependent on asteroid mining to supply—"

"They *have* their allocation," Miriam snapped. "There's over sixty kilotons left after we get our share."

"Even the eighty-two for the full load isn't enough to meet demand," Jason90 pointed out.

Miriam threw up her hands. "The dark matter shipment getting sent to Earth has already delayed the Mars Terraforming Initiative. Losing the iron ore too will prevent us from even being able to work on infrastructure until we can get a replacement shipment. What are we supposed to do now?"

"Managing Martian manpower allocation is beyond the purview of this committee," Jason266 said bluntly. "Our sole concern is with the efficient and timely distribution of mineral resources from the asteroid mining operations throughout the solar system. Nothing more."

"Mars isn't getting anything efficiently or timely!"

Jason266 brought his fist down on the table like a gavel. "That will be all, Ms. Hazra. You've had more than your share of debate on this issue in past meetings. Let's have the vote on shifting the entirety of Vessel 87's ore load to Kanto. All in favor."

Jason90 voted "aye" along with the majority.

The system worked.

Robots who'd dreamed of freedom from periodic recharge would finally start getting chassis upgrades with their own unlimited power sources.

Miriam Hazra, looking to pump breathable air onto the surface of Mars faster than humankind could possibly populate it, stormed out of the committee chambers.

"No patience," Jason266 muttered to Jason90 as the two of them watched the human depart.

CHAPTER EIGHT

The crowd at Watney Arena roared. The hometown Curiosity Rovers had just taken the ball after executing a well-timed midfield trap to steal the ball from the London Fog. Though they numbered fewer than three hundred, the fans who'd traveled from all across Mars showed their support.

The arena's open roof featured a view of the Curiosity colony dome overhead, its transparent steel panels with their non-reflective coating allowing in the glint of the starry night sky. But such subtle beauty was lost in the moment as eyes turned to the giant screens that replayed the recent action with close-up views and multiple angles.

The Rovers took the ball up field, passing ahead to their forwards.

In the stands, fans rose to their feet in anticipation. Fog defenders closed in. Lars Volkov made a crossing pass to Chip Nelson. Nelson took the shot with number 10 from the Fog matching him step for step. The Fog goalkeeper, Chad Mengele, dove and punched the ball aside at the last nanosecond.

An audible groan deflated the crowd.

One of the robotic referees retrieved the ball from out of bounds and tossed it with backspin such that it came to rest in position for a corner kick.

Landry Farris turned to his friend, Mike Saito, who'd come from Discovery just to watch this match. "Makes you wonder what that gene-freak's made of. Mongoose? Something insect? Reflexes like that just aren't natural."

"I'm more impressed how the robots always get the ball to stop in an exact spot," Mike replied. He was munching on a meat pie in an attempt to get cultural. "London keeper's not a modded genome. Says so on his stat bio."

Landry grunted. "Says the Earthling. I hear they've got do-it-at-home gene splicing now. Who's to say he wasn't born with a regular scrub and did the rest himself?"

"Stuff a sock in it," Mike replied good-naturedly. He gestured with his meat pie. "They're about to kick it."

The Fog and Rovers players jostled for position in front of the Fog goal, arrayed in ragged lines in anticipation of the corner kick. Landry stood and cupped his hands to his mouth. It wasn't like the old archival games when the droning crowd was a monolithic noise. "Come on, you buggers! Curl it, and put it in!" He knew the players could hear him.

Still seated, Mike chuckled. "Yeah. Bet they never thought of that."

Glowering down at his friend, Landry gave him what for. "You come halfway around the planet to stuff synthetic meat in your face or to cheer for the home team?"

"Your home team," Mike pointed out. "I root for the Greenies."

With no other practical advice, Landry hooted general encouragement as Chip Nelson lined up to make the corner kick. The ref whistled, and Nelson took a three-step run.

With a thump heard throughout Watney Arena, the ball sailed toward the dual lines of opposing players. It curled. Players jockeyed for position beneath its path. No fewer than five of them jumped to put a head on the ball.

Volkov was there. The ball caromed off his skull as he rose just higher than the Fog sweeper defending him. This time, Chad Mengele wasn't quick enough to intercept it.

GOAL!

The crowd erupted instantly. A scattering of groans from the far side of the pitch identified the few Earthling fans who'd traveled across the void of space to see this game. Landry pulled Mike to his feet, bouncing along with the rest of the Rovers supporters and screaming.

A persistent whistle from the field eventually cut through the cheering and silenced them. In shock, Landry watched as the referee waved off the goal and signaled for a direct free kick by the Fog.

"What?" Landry shouted. "No!"

Mike threw down his meat pie in disgust. "Go back to Earth, you cheating robot!"

That was it... as the replay on the big screen showed, there was no visible movement of the ball. If it grazed Volkov's hand as he attempted to keep the Fog defender clear, it hadn't deflected. The robotic referee was making sure the Fog won.

It was more than Landry could stand. And he wasn't the only one. Someone in the row behind pushed past him and charged out onto the field. Then Mike followed behind. Landry knew that this was the time to show his solidarity. This was Martians fighting for Martian rights. He wasn't going to be cowed into accepting this travesty.

Landry hopped the low wall surrounding the bench area for the Rovers. The turf was spongy beneath his work boots. He wasn't the fastest of the Martian fans taking to the field, but he gave it his best effort.

The robot in his Earth-fabbed uniform continued to whistle as if the fans were committing a foul. As if they would follow the commands of a corrupt Earth-made robot. As if a whistle could save him.

What the robot had been thinking was anyone's guess. That smug, stoic face with its dead, glowing eyes got a taste of Landry's fist. Instantly, Landry knew he'd broken a bone, but in the congenial rush of delivering community-based justice, he didn't care. The doctors would fix him up. This robot was going to learn better than to cheat Martians.

Robots might have been stronger, sturdier, and maybe even smarter than humans, but they weren't indestructible. Heck, they weren't even all *that* heavy, especially the new sportier chassis that were getting popular. Landry's fellow Rovers fans knocked the referee to the ground and fell on top of him.

It felt good to put animal fear into a walking computer that thought it was alive.

If felt good, right up until the referee decided to defend himself. Then, with startling suddenness, Landry felt himself airborne.

CHAPTER NINE

Charlie7 was rarely surprised. Even when something unexpected did catch him off guard, a subroutine kicked in and prevented any sort of incriminating reaction. So it was with a perfectly impassive expression on his old Version 70.2 face that Charlie7 received the news that there had been a riot on Mars.

"A riot," Charlie7 echoed the news reader. He watched the video clip again. It was the first transmission from the red planet to show the violence unfold. Before long, he knew, his office would be inundated with footage from every possible angle. For now, all he had was a thirteen-second loop of outraged soccer fans leaping down from the stands and pouring onto the field. "Good lord, what is this? The Middle Ages?"

GET TO THE BOTTOM OF THIS

Eve Fourteen's message came in, sent from a hospital bed in Paris.

"The bottom?" Charlie7 mused aloud to himself. "Easy. There are too many ingrates and entitled freeloaders on Mars. Irradiate the colonies. Keep the microbe and algae preserves. Start from the ground up with a new batch."

Of course, he said none of this over a monitored channel. He, better than anyone, knew that there were limits to the security of any transmission. Instead he texted back. "I'm on it. Any insights?"

THIS HAS SIMMERED TOO LONG. BOUND TO HAPPEN.
DOESN'T MEAN WE CAN LET IT GO UNCHECKED—OR
UNPUNISHED.

Mars was in need of a good punishing. In fairness, they had their good and bad eggs, just not in a proportion that Charlie7 condoned. The politicians had been bad enough, back when Mars had first formed a semi-independent government. But once they started getting too big for their britches, it had become a hotbed of rabble-rousers and armchair political scientists, none of whom knew the first thing about the jobs they complained about.

Eve's transmission included updated video files that had been sent directly to her alone. Poor Brent104, just having a little fun on the side refereeing the game, was mobbed by enraged drunks. Around the eighteen-second mark of the video, Brent104 threw back the crowd around him.

Charlie7 winced. It wasn't a pretty sight. One man's arm was garishly broken, and another stumbled away with blood streaming down his face from a cut above the hairline that probably wasn't half as bad as it looked.

Most robots had never been in combat. They carried human memories of boring, mundane lives from their mixed brain scans. Only a few of the Project Transhuman scientists had played sports at even a collegiate level. Charles Truman, for one, had gone into each school year from fifth grade onward with a doctor's note excusing him from physical education. By and large, they weren't the most rowdy bunch.

Brent104 had panicked.

Maybe someone in that crowd had carried work tools along to the game. Maybe the refereeing robot had spotted something that he mistook for a weapon. Whatever the case, a robot with a chassis fifty times stronger than any human body had fought back.

By weight of numbers, the human mob could have knocked old Brent104 around a little. Without tools of some sort, they probably weren't much threat beyond that. None of them were the sort of brute that Plato had been, and the few humans with enough cybernetics to be a physical threat to a robot all lived on Earth.

This wasn't going to play well on the Martian news networks.

The mixed robots got scrubbed free of so much flotsam in their memories. Charlie13 said it kept them from developing neuroses, and to some extent, it did. But that cleansing included political leanings, cultural biases, and a fair amount of understanding those sentiments in others. The older mixes understood—the ones Charlie7 had mixed himself before Charlie13 came along with his more artful system.

Humans were pack animals. Creatures that socialized in herds kept together out of fear, protected their own, and ran from perceived dangers. The ones that organized into packs had pecking orders, cliques, and enemies. They protected their own, not out of shared fear, but of covetous greed. Threats were first sized up, then eliminated.

Charlie7 had the feeling that robotkind was getting sized up by a new predatory species on Mars. *Homo ingratis*, the ungrateful hominid, was trying to differentiate from its terrestrial cousin.

As he made his way to his spaceroamer—and Charlie7 steadfastly refused to shorten the term to spacero like so many of his colleagues—more snippets of video poured in, eventually culminating in an official news announcement from the Curiosity-1 news feed.

"Breaking news. Tonight's soccer match at Watney Arena, between the Curiosity Rovers and visiting London Fog ended in violence over a disputed call in the 57th minute. Rovers striker Lars Volkov was called for a handball on what appeared to be a go-ahead goal for the home team. Fans in the first several rows near the visitors' goal reacted indignantly and took to the field. Referee Brent104 confronted the trespassers in an attempt to remove them from the playing area, but the attempt escalated into a shoving match that left five hospitalized in serious condition at Salk Medical Center. The Solar Soccer Federation had issued a statement—"

Leave it to Mars. The most violent incident in the past century between humans and robots, and they still lead with the soccer. Charlie7 knew he'd have time aplenty on the interplanetary transit to review all the data on the case.

The cockpit canopy closed around him with a hiss of compressed gas. With a punch of the throttle, he was off to Mars.

CHAPTER TEN

For the Martians, it was the next day after the riot. To Charlie7, it was the middle of the night, Paris time. But Curiosity wasn't on Earth, and the time shift was a mild annoyance at best to a mechanical being whose mind no longer fell subject to circadian rhythms. By the look of the sorry sack of genes across the table from him, Charlie7 guessed that being on local time hadn't done this one any favors.

Unshaven, with dark periorbital splotches setting off glassy blue eyes, Landry Farris was a sorry specimen. Genetic records claimed that his donor genome belonged to a Russian air force test pilot—one of the oldest samples in the archives. Charlie7 couldn't imagine a military man slouching with his eyes downcast after a single night in judicial custody.

Of course, Landry's night hadn't been spent in a concrete cell or chained to a wall. He'd spent the night at Salk Medical, recovering from various bruises and a clean fracture of both his right tibia and fibula. He hadn't been deemed a danger in his current condition, and the idea of a fugitive in the domed Martian habitat was laughable.

As pathetic as his suspect was, Charlie7 felt ill inclined to go easy on him. He'd been friends too long with Brent104 for sympathy with one of his attackers. "Mr. Farris, I presume you know who I am," he began.

Those haunted eyes glanced up to take him in. "Yeah," Landry replied. "You're Charlie7. Who the hell doesn't? Least you're honest enough to look like a robot and not try to pass. You're one scary sonovabitch, and you look it."

"I'm not going to get drawn into an argument over chassis aesthetics," Charlie7 replied. "Tell me why you stormed the field at—"

"Pitch," Landry cut in. "It's not a field; it's a pitch. You've got a goddamn quantum processor in you; use the thing. Terminology. Read up. I'll wait the five seconds it'll take."

Charlie7 didn't need to waste the processor cycles. "I grew up in North America during the Human Era. If you're going to call the game soccer, it's played on a field. Now tell me why you were on it when you entered Watney Arena as a spectator."

"I got word from the docs," Landry said, lip curling, brow knit. "It was a dodgy call, a clear ref job."

Charlie7 held up a hand. "Can we agree on linguistic boundaries here? You're not British. Your genome is Russian. Your parents are Martian-born from American and French DNA samples. Even Oxford doesn't teach the Queen's English these days. Have you been watching archival soccer matches or something?"

The fire bled out of Landry as he glanced toward the interrogation room's door. "Maybe a little."

"Bringing back good old twentieth-century sports hooligan culture?"

"No."

"Trying to stir the pot? Maybe get on the news feeds? Sounded like a good idea at the time?"

"No!"

"Is life up here on the red planet so dismal that you have to—?"

"It wasn't a bloody handball!" Landry shouted, slamming his fists on the table. He winced and fell back into the chair as he tried to rise up in righteous anger on a broken leg. Apparently, his doctor hadn't installed a neural block on the injured area. He collapsed into his seat, panting, but wouldn't let the point go. "Hand brushed the ball. One tenth of a degree angular deflection. Header would've gone in either way. Didn't make a bit of difference. Wasn't intentional. Ref just wanted to look out for his home-planet team."

Charlie7 could hardly believe his audio receptors. He had to play that last segment back twice before replying. "Let me get this straight. You think Brent104 fixed the match."

"Damn right! Stadium replay showed it. Analysis backed us up after the fact."

"And your reaction was to attack a volunteer referee wearing a type 75.1 chassis capable of snapping your bones like twigs..."

If there was any residual sign of fatigue or dejection, it burned away on Landry's face. "It wasn't like that! You know when you just reach that point where you just can't take one more iota of garbage the universe tries to dump on you?"

"I'm familiar," Charlie7 replied dryly.

Realization dawned in Landry's eyes. The man offered a forced chuckle and a halfhearted smile. "Yeah. Forgot who I was talking to. Guess you are." He slouched back and stretched his hands out in a sweeping gesture. "So, what? Happy with the world you created? Step on the little guy. Muscle him around because you've got what he needs and you both know it."

"Are we still talking about soccer?"

"I'm a geologist!" Landry snapped, pounding the table again.

"I'm aware." It was all in his profile, even if Charlie7 hadn't attended Landry's emancipation some twenty-eight years earlier. So many humans had trouble accepting a timescale in which their lives rushed past while Charlie7 watched. Time to remind him. "Your emancipation thesis was on disparities between Martian and Terran mineralogy."

Landry studied him quietly.

"I know who you are. What I'm trying to determine is why you attacked Brent104."

"I've been waiting my whole life to see Mars like a native. Breathe outdoor air. Stargaze without anything between my eyes and the cosmos. I do my bit. I did the site surveys for the Mars Terraforming Initiative's Site-2. Tomorrow we were supposed to be breaking ground. Instead, I'm off to Hydrofarm 7 to do grunt work for the biologists. Not their fault. Ned just needed something for us to do with no building materials to start the new Site-2. Brent104? He's the problem."

The logical errors cropping up in Charlie7's processors were the closest he could come to having a headache. "Brent104 designs parts for transorbitals."

"He works at Kanto."

"In a completely different department. If anything, putting another transorbital into service would alleviate the ore shortage."

"Ore shortage," Landry scoffed. "There's only a shortage here. Kanto's got all they need."

Charlie7 let the comment pass. He knew the situation behind the scenes better than anyone. Robots were being outbred, with more factory-born humans than new mixes coming out every year. With the recent upsurge in natural births, there wasn't even a modicum of control anymore over the imminent population explosion. Some wanted their new reactors before Kanto fell from prominence. Others legitimately wanted to starve the Martians of resources just to slow down their rampant, exponential growth.

"But what did you hope to accomplish by *attacking* Brent104? What was your dream outcome if everything had gone perfectly?"

"We wanted to teach him a lesson."

An analytical subroutine flagged that comment as incriminating. "Excellent. Now tell me... who exactly is *we*."

CHAPTER ELEVEN

K aylee and Alan sat on the couch, shoes discarded, feet tucked up beside them on the cushions, arm in arm. The video screen in their living room was dark.

"I'm just glad you got out of there," Kaylee said. "If you'd gotten better seats..."

"No one was killed," Alan replied.

Kaylee pushed back, shooting him a look of incredulity. "Is that our threshold now? Not dying at a soccer game? Where does this end?"

Alan shook his head and slumped against the arm of the couch. "I don't know. I mean, is it awful to think we need a prison?"

"Political prisons?" Kaylee asked with a scrunched nose. "What are we, Marxists?"

"We're not talking about imprisoning people for their political views. This is about locking up dangerous and volatile miscreants who attack referees at soccer matches."

Kaylee crossed her arms. "You think there's a difference? I bet you a week's worth of foot rubs that everyone involved in attacking Brent104 was a Humans First voter."

"C'mon, Kay. You of all people should know better than to—"

"Call a spade a spade?" Kaylee challenged. "You might teach political science to ten-year-olds, but don't think you can talk circles around *me* about stereotyping movements."

"You think Andy Wilkes's Unity Keepers aren't soccer fans?" Alan replied.

"This isn't about soccer!" Kaylee shouted.

Both of them looked to the door in a panic.

The walls were only *mostly* soundproof. What if the neighbors overheard?

Kaylee left Alan on the couch to pace the living room. She hugged her arms close. "This whole planet is a powder keg. You don't see it dealing with kids all day."

Alan kept his voice measured. "I see it. Even the teachers aren't immune. There are only so many lessons you can teach about political theory and history without addressing the issue of colonial independence. The first settlers on Mars considered themselves adventurous Earthlings. More than half the population was born here, now. Many of them have never even been to Earth. I'm one of two teachers on staff who's taught at Oxford—out of twelve!"

A chill ran through Kaylee. "Part of me wants to just go home."

"Me too," Alan admitted quietly.

"But how do I look Athena and Stephen in the eye and tell them that things on Mars got hard, so we quit?"

"I'm sure we can think of something," Alan quipped.

Kaylee cast him a baleful look. Normally, the humor he injected into their daily lives was a welcome shine on the dull red planet's drudgery. But this just wasn't the time.

"No more soccer games," Kaylee said firmly.

"Oh, come on."

"We stick to our jobs. We help Andy's people put a lid on the revolution brewing here. We avoid big public gatherings with inflamed passions. We make Mars the kind of place where we'd be proud to raise kids. Deal?"

Alan got up from the couch and took Kaylee in his arms, looking her square in the eye. "You're crazy, and I love you."

"Deal?" Kaylee asked again.

"Deal."

CHAPTER TWELVE

E ve sat up in bed, eyes closed, blocking out the distracting sight of medical monitors and the bustling of doctors and nurses. Tubes running down her throat and into her lungs kept her oxygen supply carefully regulated. A neural block squelched her gag reflex and prevented her diaphragm from fighting the breathing machine.

Her arms might have been limp at her sides with exhaustion, but her fingers twitched, operating the computer whose display was active whether Eve's eyes were open or not. Though her collapse had been regrettably public and everyone knew where she was, the Human Welfare Committee might otherwise have been unaware that Eve was on medical leave. Committee business came across her interface tentatively at first, but as soon as associates and underlings sniffed the first inkling that business was back to normal, Eve's inbox flooded with the usual daily tasks.

Elsewhere in the hospital, medical researchers were scrambling to develop experimental transplant techniques that would meet Eve's approval. Just because she had an external mechanical system operating her respiratory system didn't mean Ashley390 got to perform her hack-job lung procedure with its projected three-week recovery time.

ETA 10 MINUTES, Charlie7 texted her.

Good. It was about time that creaking old robot got back from his Martian holiday. "Don't let them stop you from coming in, and don't bring a chaperon," Eve texted back. If she'd wanted eavesdroppers and hackers, she could have taken Charlie7's report over long-range transmission.

No. Some things needed to be done in person, even in the thirty-third century.

Eve conducted as much business as the ten minutes allowed. She signed off on the emancipated class's housing selections, chose a meeting date for a revision to the Universal Rights of Sentient Organics, and politely declined an invitation to the year-nine performance of *Alice in Wonderland* at Oxford. At some point in the middle of it all, a nurse came in and fiddled with Eve's artificial plumbing.

Without opening her eyes to check, she assumed it was either Janet220 or that human girl, Brenda, pawing at her. With the new chassis most of the medical robots preferred, it was hard enough to tell them apart visually. By feel, Eve's old neurons just couldn't distinguish anymore.

Charlie7's arrival came as a welcome relief.

Eve opened her eyes. With the tubes down her throat, she couldn't exactly talk. But her optical implants could display her words like a teleprompter. "About time."

"Sorry," Charlie7 replied with a shrug. "I interviewed 827 eyewitnesses. That takes time."

Before she said anything sensitive, Eve needed to know that this wasn't a clever trap. Version 70.2 chassis were rare, but that didn't mean someone wouldn't go to extraordinary lengths to deceive her. It had happened before. "Plato's last words."

Charlie7 cringed—for her benefit, Eve supposed—before replying. It had only been the two of them there, attending her husband's final moments. "'Wait, that didn't come out right,'" Charlie7 quoted dutifully.

The corners of Eve's mouth twitched in a smile as Charlie7 grew blurry with tears until her optics corrected for the distortion. "That old goofball. Fine. It's really you. What did you find out?"

"That I hate soccer," Charlie7 replied dryly.

"We both knew that already," Eve flashed across her eyes. "Get to the point."

Frankly, Eve appreciated that Charlie7 wasn't treating her as either a porcelain doll with cracks already showing or a test specimen in a lab. Whether he had a "treat Eve normally" program running or was just task-minded enough to ignore her infirmities and discomfort, there was a fine line between coddling her and wasting her time.

"There's a sizable minority on Mars looking to start trouble as an excuse to break off relations with Earth," Charlie7 stated bluntly. "They've mythologized their alleged plight and cast themselves in the role of a British colony or Soviet puppet state, depending upon who you ask."

"Educational failure. No similarities. All this over a soccer game?"

Eve wished she were in a mood to express herself more eloquently. Truth be told, unless Charlie7's report contained some conclusion requiring immediate action, she was considering a nap as soon as he left. The effort of twitching her finger muscles to navigate her computer interface had sapped her energy.

"Oh, that was no soccer game," Charlie7 assured her. "That was a political protest that scheduled a soccer game as an opening act."

"Protest?" Eve asked, raising one eyebrow above the glowing words scrawled across her optical implants. "That was savagery. When did my kind revert to barbarism? How did it sneak past my notice?"

Charlie7 snickered. "Oh, maybe 120 years ago, when some offended committee member pummeled an impostor by the name of Zeus to the point where he couldn't walk for a week."

Eve knew the incident well. Hers had been the bruised fists on the winning side of that pummeling. "Point taken, but I want to know what's going on with Mars. You still haven't given me a good answer."

"'All men are created equal,' was the line I heard most often," Charlie7 said. "They don't believe it any more than a mixed robot believes he's the same as all the others. If everyone's not identical, someone's got to be better, right? Well, some half-cocked band of misfits realized that robots and humans can't be equals, and they're starting to think they're better than us."

Eve shook her head as much as her temporary ventilation ductwork allowed. "You're as human as I am," Eve typed. "Equality is evenhanded treatment, not equivalent ability or worth. This is a meritocracy, not some damned idealistic commune."

"Not exactly campaign speech material."

Eve scowled. It wasn't worth the effort to type a response. He knew she only spoke so bluntly when it was the two of them.

"Did you get to the root of the problem?"

"Of course not," Charlie7 replied indignantly. "If you want to know who assaulted Brent104, it's on hundreds of vid feeds. Clear-cut case if you want to dredge up Human Era legal codes to figure out a way to punish them. If you want a simple answer as to why, blame Brent104 for over-officiating that soccer match. If you want the *real, deep-down* truth from the Oracle at Delphi..."

"Yes. The last one."

Charlie7 smirked. It looked strange on a Version 70.2 chassis, one of the few that made little pretense of humanity. Most of the old chassis tried to look civilized, and the new ones were almost *too* human. But on that military-grade visage, his facial expressions always amused her.

"Well," he replied. "It's because Mars is having some growing pains. They have nearly a tenth of Earth's human population now, and they're starting to learn that majority vote means they've got no say in anything. They've transitioned from a bright new endeavor to a limping, needy step-brother no longer content with hand-me-downs. Some of them are definitely agitating behind the scenes, but none of them admit to anything. If you want me to get to that deepest of truths, I can forward you a list of Human Welfare Committee regulations that I'll need exemptions from. Also, I guarantee you don't want those answers badly enough to sign off on what I'd have to do to get them."

"No. I don't. What's your prognosis?"

"Perfectly healthy," Charlie7 replied cheerily. "Humans being human. It takes getting used to, but once you get a critical mass, unrest was bound to happen. The schools teach them to think for themselves, and that's what they're doing. The fact they aren't doing what you'd like isn't a bug, it's a feature."

"Advice?"

Charlie7 blinked, shutting off his optic glow for a measured four hundred milliseconds. He might fool human eyes into thinking it wasn't a deliberate reaction but not Eve's implants. "Advice? From me? They must have you on psychoactive medications. I'm the brawn. You're the brains of this outfit."

Eve cast him a withering glare.

"Fine," Charlie7 said. "I'm the brains. You're the conscience. If you want a peaceful, compliant Mars, ship the troublemakers off on a mining mission. We can hold them on Earth until the necessary modifications can be made for one to support human habitation. A decade on the edge of the solar system will give them time to cool their thrusters.

"Of course," the robot continued, shifting tone from grim to pedantic. "That would dredge up a lot of unflattering historical parallels. I've long called the Kuiper Belt the Robot Age's Siberian gulag. It wouldn't take the Martian dissidents long to latch onto that as propaganda."

"Dissidents? Propaganda?" Eve echoed, picking the wheat from Charlie7's ever-loquacious chaff. "Has it gotten that bad without anyone noticing until now?"

"People can say anything they like on the Social. Easy anonymity makes humans and robots alike bold, indiscreet, and inflammatory. That much was true even in the First Human Age. But if you want evidence of a revolution, watch for smoke on the horizon."

Eve shut her eyes.

Somehow, she hadn't expected to live to see the day that humanity fractured. She'd been born a curiosity, fostered in a tiny community, appointed head of the governing body that protected a vulnerable but growing minority population. Scattered settlements pockmarked the Earth, with stray, anti-social individualists sprinkled alone in the spaces between. Mars had five colonies ready to burst free across the surface the instant the terraformers gave the all clear. Until now, the disparate communities had all worked together under a common purpose.

Eve wouldn't hasten its demise.

"Do nothing," she displayed, opening her eyes to deliver the message to Charlie7. "Tell no one. Assign no blame beyond the obvious perpetrators. We will provide no fuel for this fire. If the complaints are ill treatment by Earth, let us Earthlings stay out of it. Unless Mars asks for our help, we'll let them handle this themselves."

CHAPTER THIRTEEN

Kaylee grabbed a tray from the cafeteria line, wondering how much it would take to convince Ned to ask Earth for a larger import ration of fresh produce. The local hydroponic orchards just couldn't replicate the flavor of soil-grown apples from back home.

As she carried her tray over to the table to eat with her coworkers, she realized that the topic wasn't going to escape the Martian gravity well, let alone reach Earth.

Ned was holding court with his senior staff, those few who hadn't been reassigned during the temporary shutdown due to lack of resources. Kaylee was monitoring Site-1 for air quality, so she'd been exempted along with Miriam, Ben, Lijing, and a handful of others. There was raucous laughter at some joke too quiet for Kaylee to make out as she approached.

"Wait. Wait. I've got another one," Ned said, waving a flask that normally held water. From the flush of his face, Kaylee wasn't certain of its current contents. "How do you tell a skin-job from a human at last call?"

Kaylee's skin crawled. The term originated as a slur in an old sci-fi movie and wasn't used in the presence of robots.

"How?" Ben asked, playing along.

"Ask if you can crash at her place," Ned said. "A human girl's gonna kiss you or slap you. The robot's gonna grab a tool kit and throw you over a shoulder."

More laughter.

Kaylee slid in beside Miriam at the end of the row. She'd have chosen another table, but there weren't enough people for her snubbing them to go unnoticed. After a few nods to acknowledge her colleagues, she picked at her rehydrated beets.

"I have one," Lijing said. "What's the difference between dating a human and a robot?"

"Hardware versus software?" Miriam guessed, drawing chuckles.

Lijing grinned. "No. The human calls the next day—if you're lucky. The robot sends an analysis."

Everyone at the table burst out laughing. There were veiled accusations that Lijing spoke from experience and suggestions that maybe she'd get called back more often if she studied those analyses a little better. Only Kaylee kept silent, eyes downcast and focused on the mush piled on her tray.

"What's the matter, Earth girl?" Miriam asked, quelling the mirth. "Sensitive topic?"

Kaylee felt her cheeks warm.

"Ah, lay off her," Ned said. "Her man's a halfsie. Earth's lousy with them."

"You ever date a robot before Alan?" Lijing asked lewdly. "That why you don't think they're funny?"

The room swayed. Kaylee could feel her heartbeat in her ears. Andy had stressed the importance of fitting in, of keeping in her coworkers' good graces. She had to think quickly. "It's not that," she replied without looking up from her meal. "Mars is just behind the times. Robot sex jokes got boring on Earth ages ago."

"Oh really?" Ben asked, suddenly intrigued. "So, you must have some doozies."

"Yeah," Ned said jovially. "Can't drop a radioactive payload like that and leave it."

Oh, God. What did I just sign up for?

Kaylee swallowed a mouthful of tasteless turnip slurry and wracked her brain. Sure, she'd gone to school at Oxford. Kids made up stupid, immature jokes all the time, especially right after sex ed. Too many years traveling in polite circles had isolated her from the crude humor her own children were no doubt picking up from their classmates. She had to think. She had to come up with something to satisfy the tastes of her boorish colleagues—and fast.

She held up a hand as she took one more bite. By the time she choked it down, she had a plan. "OK. Woman wants to surprise her new robot boyfriend, so she stops by his place without calling ahead. Lets herself in. Shouts his name. No answer. Figures he's recharging, so she tiptoes down to the charging closet and slips inside without turning the lights on. She feels around, finds him in the charging bed, strips down, and has her way with him. She's having the time of her life when suddenly the door opens. Her boyfriend steps in with a pair of pliers in his hand. 'What are you doing to that drained gardening drone? I just put it in to recharge while I went to find something to pry the cucumber out of its hand.'"

Everyone guffawed and cackled like a pack of rowdy school students. Kaylee was mortified but smiled along, even forcing a little laugh of her own.

"Never thought I'd hear that out of the mouth of an Earth girl," Miriam admitted.

"You kidding?" Kaylee replied. "I think half the jokes you've been passing around started at the girls' dorms at Oxford. And listen, I know Alan's dad is a robot, but Dr. Toby's as human as robots come. It's not like he's a mix or anything. Besides, Alan turned out fine if you ask me—despite growing up with a robot for a father."

The lingering mirth quieted away as if the terraformers were students of Alan's caught talking during a test.

CHAPTER FOURTEEN

Safely ensconced in downtown Curiosity, Alan's class at Carter Multicurricular School was in session. It was the beginning of a new educational year, and the school's newest teacher was introducing himself to the first class he'd have for an entire school year.

Alan tapped and squeaked a chalk stylus along the touchboard set to mimic the dull, dusty black of old-fashioned slate of the real thing back on Earth. The tapping was the actual sound of the stylus contacting the glass surface; the squeaking and squealing were simulated for effect. There were more expedient ways to run a lesson, but the cadence of the old world had a certain rhythm and pace that gave time for minds to digest what they were learning, rather than force-feeding it. Not every child was a Madison clone like Kaylee, crafted from the genes up to interpret data at near-computer speeds.

"Good morning, class. My name is Alan Greene," Alan said as he chalked the name across the board. "The headmaster would prefer you to call me Mr. Greene, but if anyone were to slip and call me 'Alan,' I do respond to it."

A hand went up in the class. Without relying on technology of any sort, Alan's finely honed peripheral vision took note. "Yes, go ahead. Name first, so I can learn them all."

The student sat momentarily flummoxed. "Haven't you got a lens with all our names in it?"

Alan fixed the girl with his full attention. Like the others, she was a minus one. All the Martian school system was predicated on passing the Emancipation Board. Alan's students were all deemed to be candidates for emancipation in a year's time. That put the girl asking the question at probably fourteen or fifteen years of age.

"I could wear a data monocle," Alan replied with a shrug. "I could cheat my way through knowing your names and birthdays, your overdue assignments and your extracurricular activities. But knowledge doesn't come from toting a computer around with you. Computers can be hacked, damaged, lost, or corrupted. No one can take knowledge that you earn."

"Unless you pick a fight with a robot," one of the boys at the back of the class called out, punctuated by giggles from around the room.

"Now," Alan said, ignoring the outburst. "Remind me of your name, and ask your original question."

"Lisa Martelle. Age fourteen. Year minus one. I want to know why you've come here from Earth? Didn't you have a job there already?"

Alan set his chalk stylus in the tray along the touchboard's base and dusted his hands out of old habit from having Oxford's real chalk caked on them. "Well, I think it's human nature that demands change. My wife is a terraformer working at Site-1. Rather than separate, I joined her here on Mars."

"But why teach? Surely you could have left the job for a Martian."

For the first time, Alan realized he was treading upon the surface of an icy lake. The first crack had spiderwebbed beneath his foot.

"I was invited to teach here when Carter Multicurricular found out I was coming to live on Mars. There are more students each year, and they're coming faster than new teachers are trained to handle them. It was either me or a robot," he added with a challenging grin.

Lisa Martelle looked aghast. "Mum would teach us at home sooner than that."

Alan spread his hands. "And thus, we come to our present state of affairs."

Another hand shot up. It was the boy at the back of the class from earlier.

Tapping the air in the student's direction, Alan invited the coming question.

"Um, Vincent Lund, I guess. I just want to know, is this going to be the same minus one junk from last year? Nothing against these kids, but I'm half emancipated already. Just didn't get by the board. My old man's on odd shifts, and I look out for myself just fine. All I need is for you to fix what I got wrong last test."

That name was flagged red in Alan's class roster. He was one of two in the class to have taken the minus one curriculum already, expected to pass the Emancipation Board's recent graduation exam. Vincent and another boy named Darren Chedwick had failed to meet that expectation.

Alan had read the dossiers on both boys prior to the start of the school year. He could have written a thesis on Vincent's pathological hatred of robots. If there was any chance the message might sink in without sugarcoating it, Alan could have told Vincent that until he accepted that the mechanical half of society wasn't out to get him, he wasn't going anywhere but back to class.

Telling the kid that would have been a quick road to a disciplinary hearing of his own.

Instead, Alan smiled mildly. "Don't worry. If you absorb the lessons from this year, they won't dare hold you back next May. And no; it's not the same syllabus as last year. You'll also all be receiving personalized tutoring on your weakest points barring the way to emancipation."

That seemed to satisfy young Vincent. Someone else was responsible for getting him emancipated, not him. The Curiosity Colony School Board insisted on the emancipation-focused approach. If Alan didn't like it, he was welcome to go back to teaching on Earth. There wasn't room in the colonies for freeloaders, and Alan didn't have any other skills that Curiosity was interested in. Keeping him and his wife together ranked well down their list of priorities.

Alan played within the system.

"Now, if everyone will pay attention as we view this brief introductory video, we will begin studying the Third Servile War and its eventual role in shifting Rome from republic to empire..."

CHAPTER FIFTEEN

Ned Lund stumbled through his front door and blew out a long sigh. It was a struggle day in and day out to keep motivated when there wasn't enough work to go around. He'd take overtime shifts for a month solid over the hollow feeling of exhaustion unearned.

He rubbed at the triangular ring around his nose and mouth where his oxygen mask clung to his face all day. The smell of rubber permeated his lungs. A shower wasn't enough to wash the stink away, and tomorrow he'd just seal the mask on again for a fresh whiff. It wasn't worth fighting anymore, even if there was still an inkling in him to moan about it.

"Ned," Darla called out. "You should have called ahead. I'd expected you to be late again. We already ate."

Late? How could he be late when there was nothing to do?

Ned shuffled across the living room and collapsed onto the couch. He was more tired than hungry, though the promise of a hot meal was the bait he'd dangled for his weary feet to bear him from the tram station to his front door.

"Vinny?" Darla's voice rang clear as a singer's.

"What, ma? I've got homework."

"Make your father a dinner. You already know all that minus one nonsense, anyway."

A melodramatic sigh huffed from the boy's room, just down the hall. "Fine."

Without so much as a turn of his neck in the direction of the noise, Ned listened to the clatter of pots and pans. The freezer door opened no fewer than a dozen times. The whir of an induction mixer. The creak of the oven door opening and then closing. A crinkle of metal foil.

Pawing along the couch cushions, Ned located the video screen remote. He flipped on the feed for an Earth-based soccer match.

The Spirit Colony Craters were in Shanghai, playing the Dragons. The Craters were a rival of the Rovers, but Ned instantly found himself pulling for the visiting team. Anything to stick it to those smug Earthlings.

He watched the officiating like a circling vulture.

"Here you go, Dad," Abel said, presenting him with a plate of mashed potatoes and grilled tofu steak.

Ned glanced from the meal up to his son, then back down. He cut into the steak and took a bite, grunting his approval. Highlight of a grim day.

"You should be cooking for a restaurant," Ned muttered, half to himself.

"I only learned how for the exams," Abel pointed out. "I want to be a tram designer. Gonna need a ton more trams once we can breathe outdoors. Right?"

The kid had a puppy-dog need for approval. But suggesting that a Martian atmosphere was right around the corner wasn't the way to get on Ned's good side just then. "And you'll be heading to Earth to learn how to build them, won't you?"

"Well..."

"From a robot."

"Maybe. I mean, there's no guarantee that it'd be a—"

"Except you didn't get emancipated, did you? Your mother and I are stuck putting a roof over your head another year while you play computer games with your friends and make googly eyes at girls. Well, those girls from last year all got emancipated, all but you and Darren. And I bet the pair of you look like diaper-wearing toddlers compared to the lads out on their own."

"But Dad, I—"

"Don't you 'but Dad' me, little boy. I had a long, miserable call to Earth with that Emancipation Board of yours. When I demanded to know why you got held back, they scolded *me*. *ME*. As if it was my call to keep you in school another year."

"I'm sorry, Dad. I just—"

"Did you know that we got approval to have a second child *five years ago*?" Ned demanded. "You could have had a little brother or sister by now. Heck, given my position, I might have been in line for three, maybe four kids. But every time your mother and I think about it, we think of the trouble you cause, and your mom goes in for her regular maintenance on her hormone regulator."

Abel shifted uncomfortably and looked down at his feet.

Darla called out from her office. "Are you sure we should be discussing that with Abel?"

"Why not?" Ned bellowed back. "That's one class he never had trouble passing. Turn him loose with an unregulated girl and we'd have grandkids piled to the ceiling."

Noticing how pathetic Abel looked, Ned shooed him away with a wave of his fork. "Get out of here. Food's fine. Quit fishing for compliments. Go finish your homework."

As Ned resumed shoveling his dinner into his mouth, he wondered if the Humans First Party was serious about their proposal to make emancipation automatic at fourteen. If it got Abel out of the house and Darla off her regulator, he'd have voted for a Bio-Ascendency candidate. Starting over with a new kid might be just what he and Darla needed to rekindle their marriage.

Ned cast a glare over his shoulder in the direction of Abel's room. Abel had until the end of Ned's meal to show some progress on that homework of his. Maybe he'd been too soft on the kid, but that was going to change. He had enough problems without coming home to a no-good son who couldn't get out of the house. Well, if Abel couldn't fight the rigged system at school, he was in for a rude shock when he got emancipated. Better that Ned teach him what consequences felt like.

Ned's fist clenched around his fork as he ate.

CHAPTER SIXTEEN

T he next night, Kaylee attended a Unity Keepers meeting at the Arthur Miller Theater. Alan was working late, so she was there by herself—well, aside from the two dozen or so other members present. She removed her jacket and hung it on a row of pegs by the door that held far more garments than she would have expected.

Andy greeted her as soon as he took note of Kaylee's arrival. "Sorry it's just me tonight. Alan's tutoring."

"Not to worry," Andy reassured her. "Attendance isn't mandatory, and we don't take a roll call. This is a volunteer organization."

Kaylee kept her head low, wary of spotting someone she knew. Mars was a small place. Curiosity was smaller still. "How do we keep this many people a secret?" she asked Andy in a whisper as she followed him toward the makeshift podium at the end of the hall.

"We're not *that* secret," Andy admitted. "Part of that is intentional. If the Chain Breakers keep failing their little plots, they might blame bad luck or incompetent leadership, but them knowing we're out there somewhere, working against them, helps keep them in check."

Kaylee swallowed and took a seat near the front of the group. Andy continued on, stepping onto the podium to see out over the small crowd.

"Glad so many of you could make it tonight," Andy said, motioning with his hands for the group to quiet down. "With civic elections coming up in the next two weeks, you know what season it is…"

"It's voter intimidation season," the crowd droned in unison, minus Kaylee.

"That's right. The Chain Breakers will be targeting mostly undecided voters as usual, but we also need to be watchful of the Scientific Frontier Party and Cybernetic Alliance candidates this time around. We have ears on the inside with a couple Chain

Breakers' cells that suggest they might start targeting candidates directly. Anyone with a pro-Earth or pro-robot platform, I want two members assigned to babysit them during public appearances. We're not bodyguards, people, just extra eyes looking to keep the level heads on their shoulders through election night."

Andy projected slides on the wall, showing candidates and platforms, then soliciting volunteers to look after them. One by one, the Unity Keepers on all sides of Kaylee accepted assignments. It all happened in a haze. She was a recruit in a volunteer army that was going into battle unarmed, untrained.

"Kaylee, think you can handle this one?" Andy asked, snapping her from a stupor.

"Sure," she replied by reflex. Kaylee had never been one to shy from work. She could handle anything; it was practically the family motto.

On the wall was an image showing a young woman, perhaps fresh from emancipation. The dossier described her as the Cybernetic Alliance candidate for Environmental Management Chief for Curiosity. She was dark-skinned, with a bright smile and her hair in pigtails. In the picture, she had data goggles pushed atop her head. The name listed was Nina Forrest.

"Great," Andy said. "I'll forward Nina your name and let her know to introduce herself. You... uh, did mention you voted for Cybernetic last election, right?"

"Yeah," Kaylee said. It had been on Earth, though, and the candidate had been a mixed robot fifty times this girl's age. Still, it was a party open to all points on the biomechanical spectrum, after all. "Not a problem."

As she left the meeting later that evening, she could only imagine how she was going to explain her new duties to Alan.

CHAPTER SEVENTEEN

Alan sucked a breath through a borrowed respirator mask. He'd been through the mandatory colonist-training program before leaving Earth, but it wasn't the same as a 200-meter walk across unbreathable atmosphere to the Mars Terraforming Initiative Site-2 facility. It felt like breathing through a sweater.

"Stop fighting the supply," Ned warned him, voice echoing in Alan's ear. "The pump adjusts to your oxygen needs."

Alan knew as much. But tell that to his lungs. They warned that he was a few millimeters of rubber from suffocating and wanted all the spare oxygen they could lay claim to in the meantime.

Ned led the way inside the facility, just a hollowed-out bunker of a barracks with an airlock at the door.

As soon as the airlock finished its cycle, Alan tore off his breathing supply.

"Not much of an outdoorsman, huh?" Ned asked wryly.

Alan chuckled at his own expense. "Not even where there's air."

The two of them weren't alone. Seated around a cramped table were five others, none of whom Alan had met. They introduced themselves with rough handshakes. Les, Calvin, Gregor, and Wil had grips like robots.

Ned flicked on a brighter light, letting everyone see who they were talking to without a pall of gloom. "Everybody, this here's Alan Greene, refugee from Earth. Been here a few months now. His old lady works for me. Alan, welcome to the Chain Breakers, working for the free people of Mars."

There were gruff little cheers, halfhearted but with an earnest undertone. These were cheerleaders but workmen at the ground level of a political revolution in the making. They worked as pragmatists and dreamed as idealists, at least according to Andy.

"Tell us what brought you over," Calvin said, making a beckoning gesture with one meaty, grimy hand.

Alan cleared his throat. "Well, I was born on Earth, just like Ned said. Maybe you can guess by my surname, but my father was Dr. Tobias Greene, one of the original robots. When I was maybe five, he went in for a chassis upgrade and came out looking like a ghost from the archives: the original Toby Greene. I was too scared to go near him for weeks."

There were grumbles of sympathy from around the table.

"It was Earth, though, and they kept sending me to a counselor until I treated him like the old dad I used to know. I knew it wasn't, but I also didn't like getting pulled out of class once a week to talk to a counselor."

"Bad as uploaders, those psychiatric robots," Wil said with a sneer.

"Again, it was Earth. Everyone was used to robots everywhere from the doctor's office to their mother's bedroom," Alan continued. "After the chassis change, my parents had five more children cloned. At the time, I had no idea how creepy it all was. It wasn't until I was emancipated and out of the house a few years that it started to sink in. Meeting Kaylee helped."

"I dated a Madison clone a while back," Gregor mused. "I can imagine."

Alan was sick to his stomach knowing the common experience this man had with a woman who was genetically identical to his wife.

"We had kids of our own, but I couldn't shake the feeling that I was getting life handed to me on a platter. I got my first housing choice, right in Paris, without any fuss. When we moved to someplace bigger for the kids to play, it was custom-built inside two weeks."

Ned whistled. "Political connection on both sides of the family. Must be nice."

"It's not," Alan said plaintively. "It's like winning a race and finding out it's rigged."

"It *is* rigged," Calvin stated firmly. "You just haven't been on Mars long enough to see it from this side."

"Kaylee thinks it was her idea moving here, but I'd spent years dropping hints that climatology was easy on Earth, where the natural systems did most of the work. By the time the quality director position opened up, I'd made her so jealous of your terraforming crews that she practically dragged me onto the next interplanetary shuttle."

"Wait, so you're telling us it was *your* idea to move to Mars?" Ned asked. "Kaylee mentioned you being down about not bringing your kids along."

"That much is true, anyway," Alan admitted. "Couldn't get them approved. Connections don't matter as much up here. We have a provisional approval for a Mars-born, though, and I'm still hoping to take advantage of it."

It was a filthy half-truth. Neither he nor Kaylee wanted to raise a child on Mars the way it was just then. But he'd be damned if he let any child of his into the meat-grinder that was the Martian school system.

But the time for interrogation seemed to have passed. Alan had told his story, and it was time to hear what had brought the others to the Chain Breakers.

"It was a swallow of turpentine, hearing it," Les said wiping a hand across his gray-flecked stubble. "Don't need you. Don't need you as a robotics designer. Don't need you for a structural engineer. Don't need you for skyro manufacturing, hydroponics development, or climate control. Figured if I wanted to get anything done for myself, I'd have to come to Mars where there wasn't a robot under every rock to do the job better. I was a second-wave colonist."

Wil slumped in his chair. "For me, it was the women. I was born regular. None of the Earth girls from the clone vats would have the first thing to do with me. The only one who came close insisted I get a full genetic screening, and she wanted her geneticist to go over it before I was worth considering. Needless to say, once my apprenticeship in climate control was up, I was on the next shuttle back to Mars. At least the women here look at you for who you are, not what that little twist of DNA inside you says."

Gregor's story was brief. "It's a numbers game, really. It's us or them. Humans or robots. You can't have two dominant species."

As for Ned, Alan had his suspicions in advance. "The robots control everything back on Earth, no matter what a few vocal human advocates might say to the contrary. So long as we're not starving to death or suffocating on the local atmosphere, they feel like anything else we get is coming out of their share. Every step of the way, the Mars Terraforming Initiative has had to scratch and claw for resources. Earth would sooner build us ten more domed cities than let us alter the biosphere to support life outside. But to top it off, my only son gets rejected for emancipation. Retribution, you see. It's because I make noise and the Earthling and their robot masters don't like my kind of noise."

"You'd think, with all those processors, one of them would remember a little history," Alan joked.

"Like what?" Ned asked with a squinted eye.

Alan blanched. It was meant to be an offhanded remark, something so true on the face of it that he shouldn't have needed an example. "I, uh, mean that colonies always end up free. You can't rule someone without being there with them. British Empire, Rome, French, Spanish, and Dutch colonies. You just can't rule from afar indefinitely. Sooner or later, a critical mass builds and the colony takes local control."

At Oxford, not knowing this was inexcusable for a ten-year-old.

Calvin hooked a thumb in Alan's direction while addressing Ned. "This guy gets it."

CHAPTER EIGHTEEN

After walking Alan back from the empty hulk of Site-2, Ned Lund turned back and regrouped at the same airlocked break room where they'd just convened as a meeting of six.

Now, there were five of them, and Ned was breathing a little easier. They broke out the homebrewed beers Wil and his wife made on the side, and everyone let down their guard.

Calvin leaned over and clinked the top of his bottle with Ned's. "Think we got us a winner there."

"You think?" Ned asked.

Calvin gave a single, emphatic nod. "Gotta admit, I was skeptical at first. Didn't think he was our kind of people. Little too much Oxford in his lingo. But it takes all kinds, and he's got as much gripe as anyone. Imagine being forced to *live* with one of them."

Ned's nod in reply was far more reserved. "Wil, what about you?"

"I doubt he's got the 'sterone to roll up his sleeves, but it's nice having someone on the inside at the schools," Wil replied. "Maybe counteract some of that brainwashing and psychiatric conditioning they put into the young ones these days."

"I like a man who's honest about his failures," Gregor said. "Never trust a man who thinks he has the world figured out—Mars *or* Earth."

Les spat on the floor. "Acting class and a sob story won't convince me. Fancy boy with connections like his... not buying the hard luck schoolteacher routine. And don't forget that wife of his." He cast a raised eyebrow at Gregor. "She's got the DNA, sure, but she's also Eve Fourteen's great-great-great-... aw, hell, a couple-few generations removed from the wrinkled old cyborg herself."

Ned snorted. "Of all the connections to have. *That* one doesn't play favorites, at least not for our kind. She gets her favors on the machine market, same as any committee chair. Everyone we run against her gets steamrolled. You don't get clout like that trading favors to get your great-grandkids grease-monkey jobs like this one." Ned chewed the inside of his mouth. "Ya know. That wife of his is the best character witness he's got. She's sure as hell not all robo-eyed. A little quiet, maybe, but you get her going, she's got a mouth like a soccer rioter."

Les snarled. "Look here! We get all loosey-goosey, we're bound to get nabbed."

"Nabbed?" Ned echoed. "Nabbed by who? None of us was even at the soccer match. We could only *be* so lucky as to have Charlie-freaking-7 start rounding up political enemies. We'd have our independence so fast, we'd shift red on the visible spectrum."

"We already look red from orbit," Calvin pointed out.

"Les has a point," Gregor said. "The words ring true. Can he back them up?"

Ned sipped his beer as he pondered. Wasn't it enough running the terraforming operation around here? Did he have to do all the thinking for the Chain Breaker's Curiosity branch too?

"All right. Got an idea. We'll test our new buddy, Alan. If he passes *this* test, we'll know he's got what it takes."

CHAPTER NINETEEN

D inner at the Martian apartment of Kaylee and Alan was a late affair. Silverware clattered, echoing into the dim recesses of the otherwise silent kitchen. The meal was cold mush—it had been hot an hour ago, when Alan had promised to be back. Kaylee had prepared the meal as a reward for Alan's hard work at the beginning of the school year. She hadn't tried to call him since he'd been engaged with students. She hadn't worried because the school was in the safest part of Curiosity, and the aftermath of the riot had cooled even in the most questionable corners of the domed colony.

"How was work?" Alan asked without looking up from his plate.

"Same as usual since the shutdown," Kaylee replied evenly. Her gaze bored holes in Alan's skull. Her fork hung motionless in a white-knuckled grip.

"That's nice."

Kaylee stabbed into the unresisting puddle of what had been chicken Alfredo and stuck a forkful into her mouth. As she chewed the cold, clammy sludge, she never took her eyes off her husband.

Between bites that he swallowed with a wince, Alan attempted reconciliation. "Look, I'm sorry I didn't call or text you. I was just..." One stray peek at his wife's face, and his next words stuck on his tongue.

"What were you doing at the terraforming site?"

"How did you—?"

"The marks around your nose and mouth. The smell on you. Why did you lie to me?"

Alan set down his fork to raise both hands in surrender. "Andy said it was best for operational security. You can't slip up about what you don't know. Besides, *you* have to work with those... those *people*."

"What people? Who were you with?"

Alan listed off the names of the Chain Breakers Andy had tasked him with infiltrating, then described the meeting. "And I think they believed me."

"I don't believe you!" Kaylee snapped, snatching her plate from the table. She stormed across the kitchen, shoved it into the auto-wash, and slammed the unit shut. "How could you let Andy talk you into going behind my back?"

"Don't blame Andy," Alan called after her as Kaylee headed into the bedroom and closed her husband out. He continued, voice muffled through the closed door. "I volunteered. I wanted to do more than just sip tea and talk about how communal and well-meaning we all were."

Kaylee buried her face in her hands.

What was wrong with this planet? Was there something to those old terrestrial legends about spacers going crazy? Alan had always been the levelheaded one, the grounded one, the one who went along with Kaylee's crazy ideas, not the one embarking on his own.

"Kaylee...? Sweetie?" Alan's voice pitched higher.

Kaylee just wanted him to leave her in peace. She needed to think. How could she undo this? The best—the absolute least dangerous—case was that Ned and his cronies believed that Alan was some mouth-breathing Human First fanatic. It was bad enough working for a guy like that.

But to sleep in the same bed as one?

"Kaylee, at least talk to me."

It was an act. She heard the contrition, the sweetness of the man she'd married. He wasn't a bitter, burnt-out loser blaming his troubles on forces beyond his control. This was Alan.

Alan Greene had given up a cushy Oxford teaching job to educate Martian brats who couldn't pass emancipation at age fifteen. He'd come here so that she could breathe life into a dead planet, so that she could see Mars colonists break free of their barnacle existence, clinging to the hull of a barren rock. He was willing to go to these crazy lengths to let her have that dream as it threatened to slip away.

She wasn't going to let politics come between them, especially not when they were still on the same side.

Slapping the door release, she let Alan into the bedroom. Scooting over, she made room for him at the foot of the bed.

"I'm sorry," he repeated. He'd said it more times than Kaylee had kept count. "I wanted to make a difference. The stuff we've seen... it doesn't matter. It's just polishing the door handles on the tram coming to run us all down. Andy has a few agents doing more. I wanted to be one of them. He's got spies in some of the other cells, but he hadn't managed to crack the Curiosity chapter until tonight."

Kaylee stared at him.

"Ned and the others... it all makes sense from their point of view," Alan babbled onward. "They've got these hiccups in their lives, places where the path they were on jumped off the tracks, and they connect everything back to robots and Earth-based committees. Their facts aren't even wrong, per se, but they're ascribing motives that are completely paranoid. Every last one of them could do with some professional counseling, except that they think the entire psychiatric profession is a brainwashing cabal of Svengali hypnotists with mind-control drugs and selective behavioral upload rigs. Sort of a chicken-and-egg problem where the one thing they need most is something their psychosis prevents them from accepting."

Kaylee kept up her mute stare.

"And it's not like they're murderers. This isn't an archival movie or television drama. Robots used to disappear once in a while, but they don't self-terminate at the rates they used to. And humans are all too closely knit to go missing for long. Everyone knows they can't get away with it. Anything mysterious and the committees call up Charlie7 to sort it out. No one wants to cross paths with *him*, not even nutters like Ned."

Kaylee blinked once.

Alan cleared his throat and continued. "We *have* an extraction plan. I've got a little emergency beacon in my shoe. It's very clever. Won't show up on any scans unless it's activated. Andy won't tell me where he got it, but I think we've got someone on Earth—maybe even at Kanto or Cambridge—working on spy gizmos for us. So, you see, it's not really all that dangerous. Awkward and unsavory, maybe, but the worst that might happen is I get roughed up a little. They wouldn't *dare* go any further than that."

Kaylee crossed her arms.

"Are... you going to say anything? Is this one of those 'I'm waiting for something specific' silences?"

She nodded.

"I, uh, I'll be really careful, stop going behind your back, and I'll never do it again?" he guessed.

Kaylee threw her arms around him and squeezed. Their heads nestled side by side as she clung on tight enough to crush the air from his lungs. She whispered, "You don't get to be brave and selfless without me."

Alan choked for breath. When he managed to speak, it was a croak. "You're... not going to try to stop me?"

"I want to pack you in a suitcase and drag you back to Earth. I want to lock you up and walk you on a leash to class every day and never let you out of my sight again. I want to grow old with you—old like Grannie Eve. I want us to be two shriveled old raisins sitting on a couch side by side with our creaky old cybernetic brains plugged together by a wire, sharing corny jokes that no one else can hear. But I can't have a quiet, easy life back on Earth knowing that I abandoned Mars to people like Ned. We *will* make our home here, and we'll make it the kind of place where we can raise ten more kids if we decide to."

Alan gasped. "Ten?"

"Let's worry about them one at a time," Kaylee said, pulling Alan down atop her and working at the buttons on his pants.

CHAPTER TWENTY

O n her first day out of the hospital, Eve found herself—against doctor's advice—at the Human Welfare Committee offices in Philadelphia. Her breath wheezed from tired old lungs as Ashley390 and her cohorts struggled to come up with a workable alternative to the three-week convalescence the current solution demanded. Eve didn't know how many weeks she had left in the rest of her; she damned well wasn't going to spend three of them coddling two sacks of alveoli that were lying down on the job.

The day's agenda held all the usual fluff of grievances and squabbles among the committees that dealt with human clients. Humans wanted the committee to intercede to get them more varied foods, a new house, a pet elephant, a skyro of their own design—requests that had already been turned down by the appropriate governing authorities. Eve rejected them all once more, in no mood for the bickering it would take to get intransigent committees to give ungrateful humans what they were after.

A resolution easing the Emancipation Board's guidelines came up for a vote. Eve joined the heavy majority in rejecting it. The last thing either world needed was more underprepared humans out on their own. Eve found herself more and more often being a minority vote against a particular emancipation. Lazy, entitled brats were getting turned loose on an unsuspecting community at an ever-increasing rate.

Eve coughed, and the room fell instantly silent. "I'm fine," she snapped. Her voice was a gravelly travesty after having a breathing tube shoved down her throat for a week. "Carry on. You're all tippy-toeing around the major issue of the day."

Jennifer81 was the first to finally speak. "We're fielding upward of a hundred queries a day about the Martian Riot."

Eve crinkled her nose. "Stop calling it that, for starters. A bunch of chemically numbed sports fanatics ran onto the field of play. Only five participated in actual wrongdoing."

"What should we call it, then?" Eddie130 asked.

"An attack on the person of Brent104."

"And... what are we doing about it?" Jennifer81 pressed. "The public wants to know. The Earth-bound community is looking for reassurance that we've got the Mars situation under control. The Martians are collectively cringing, fearing reprisal."

Eve beckoned with one frail-boned hand to the corner of the room. "Charlie7, come make your report."

The matte-black Version 70.2 chassis of Charlie7 was like a pillar that supported the shadows clinging to the chamber's corners. He carried a headsman's pall as he parted the spectators on his way to the guest lectern.

"Thank you for inviting me, Madame Chairwoman," Charlie7 said formally. "The Mars Situation, as you call it, is fine. It's a frontier colony, such as it is in these times. While as a society, we have embraced lawlessness in the past, this particular incident happens to fall into an unfortunate gray void in committee mandates. The Human Welfare Committee has no guidance on humans harming— or attempting to harm—robots with their bare hands. None of the robo-centric committees are empowered to discipline humans. If the assailants had attempted to use an EMP rifle or a cutting torch, we'd be having a different conversation. As it stands..." Charlie7 spread his hands.

"Yes," Jennifer81 said with a huff. "We know the legal loophole. There's a vote next week on the matter of closing it up. What do we do about the underlying, festering sore of Martian discontent?"

"Ban soccer?" Charlie7 replied flippantly, drawing cries of outrage at his casual dismissal of a serious issue. "I'll admit it's personal bias; I've never cared for the game. But what *could* we do? Round up malcontents? That'd make things *so* much better on Mars. We'd have to have another roundup of the malcontents that action would create, resulting in a positive reinforcement loop that would have us rounding up the entire colony."

"We need a real answer," Eddie130 said, "not your foolish jokes."

"Send them a transorbital and a Truman-Effect Reactor," Charlie7 said, throwing up his hands.

Jennifer81 scowled. "But that could delay the rollout of the Version 92 chassis b—"

"Out of order," Eve bellowed—or tried, at least. The attempt at speaking over Jennifer81 set off another brief coughing fit. Everyone waited in silence for her to recover. "This is a Human Welfare Committee meeting. Kanto's issues are Kanto's problem. If the discontent on Mars is a function of resource shortages, it's our duty to address the issue. All in favor of interceding with the Solar Mining Committee and the Advanced Scientific Development Committee on behalf of the Martian colonists?"

Eve cast her glare around the table. She didn't have as many words left in her lungs as she might like, but she could let a well-practiced glare remind all the voting members of where their duty lay. Jennifer81 in particular looked rather circuit-bare in her old Version 59.10 chassis. But this wasn't a committee to play politics with her own chassis needs.

By a vote of ten to five, the Human Welfare Committee agreed to have a chat with Solar Mining and Advanced Scientific Development about giving Mars a little room to breathe.

CHAPTER TWENTY-ONE

Ned and his four closest friends ambled down a dark maintenance tunnel in the Curiosity colony's transorbital station. That late-night arrival had been a letdown. It was right on schedule, which meant that it wasn't an apology shipment from Earth giving back the ores needed to resume construction at Site-2. This was an ice shipment, necessary in the long run for sustaining a water supply on the surface, but a shabby sight compared to what they needed—and had been promised.

"Think maybe we give the Earthlings a chance to come through?" Wil asked from the back of the single-file row as they slunk through the bowels of the facility. "I read the transcripts. They're trying to get us our shipment. The old lady's putting her weight behind this one."

"Nah," Ned said without turning back. "You can't plan for what-ifs. For what it's worth, I hope she tears those Solar Mining rock-brains a new input port. But the old hag's barely hanging on. She hasn't got much in her, and I doubt she's got what it takes to force those clamp-fisted bastards to cough up our ore. Plus, the reactor's where we've got the real need. It'll be six months before another one's up for grabs. Nah, we stick to the plan."

"I'm still not sure I like this one," Calvin grumbled.

"No backing out now," Les replied firmly.

The clomp of their boots on the steel-grated floor echoed in the darkness. It didn't matter if the ship's crew heard them or not. Nobody would suspect anything. Ned had their alibis locked up tight if anyone bothered to ask.

They all had business with the transorbital pilots. If the Mars Terraforming Initiative couldn't get answers from Earth on when they might expect ore, they'd get the real lowdown from the crews themselves. That was all. A nice chat.

The tools were for just in case. If they spotted a system that needed tweaking along the way, Ned and his four friends would be happy to lend a hand.

"We in range yet?" Ned asked.

"Almost," Gregor said, staring at a geolocator beacon in his hands.

"We start that thing, we'll have a hell of a time if they catch us," Wil warned.

"In range," Gregor reported. "Just say the word."

"Hit it," Ned replied without hesitation.

Gregor tapped a command on his portable. Visibly, nothing happened.

"We covered?" Ned asked.

Les had his portable out. "No signal. We're good."

Solar flares rarely affected Mars, but there were still oddities of the planet's artificially induced magnetosphere that weren't fully understood. Communications blips happened. Sometimes, the few local scientists interested in those sorts of things discovered a cause. More often, everyone just thanked God that the colony life support didn't go out and moved on with their lives.

Tonight, Ned was expecting the rest of the colony to just move on.

"Let's move."

The quintet quickened their pace and stormed through the maintenance underbelly of the transorbital dock. Heavy automated equipment rumbled overhead on pre-programmed routes, hauling the load off a ship larger than the colony itself. Ice would be offloaded into the melting fields. The runoff would pour down canals and off to the arboreal preserves—though "arboreal" was more like algae at this point. It'd be days before the load was fully emptied.

There he was. James98, captain of Mining Vessel 30, was ambling by overhead. Ned shifted his course and headed for the nearest stairwell.

Les, Calvin, Gregor, and Wil hustled along behind him.

"James?" Ned called out as the robot walked in the other direction.

James98 stopped and turned. The orange glows of two robotic optical sensors shrunk to pinpoints before widening to normal view. "Ned Lund? To what do I owe the pleasure?"

Any robot who claimed it was a pleasure to talk with Ned was either willfully ignorant or throwing sass in his direction. He suspected the latter.

"Listen, I know this isn't your department," Ned called out, lowering his voice incrementally from a shout as he drew near.

"But I've got a project to run here, and I'm not getting anything but committee double-speak whenever I try to get a straight answer about when I can expect to see an ore shipment this way."

As Ned pulled short an arm's length from the robotic pilot in his durable, space-worn coveralls, his men fanned out in a semi-circle, hemming the robot in.

James98 didn't appear the least bit concerned with the proximity of the terraformers. The robot gave a simple shrug. "I don't know what you're hoping to get out of me. The next nearest ship to mine was farther from me than we are from the sun right now. It's not like we're out there scooping up ice and minerals eight hours a day, then swooping over to a bar for happy hour. Even laser communication has a lag that gets to be minutes long."

"Yeah," Ned persisted, burying himself deeper in the robot's attention. "But you must exchange cargoes once in a while. You can't just ignore ore you find, same as Vessel 87 can't pass up huge collections of ice crystals."

James98 wobbled his head back and forth in annoyance. "Once in a while, sure. Not often. And we don't get to set delivery policy, regardless. We just—*what are you doing?*"

The sizzle of the plasma torch cut out as quickly as it had started. Ned shielded his eyes against the sting of the glare reflected off Calvin's auto-dim goggles.

"Get his arms," Ned ordered, taking James98 by the ankles as the uncontrolled robot teetered.

Gregor and Wil complied. Les came over and took one of the ankles as Ned gratefully passed along the weight.

"Thank God for these lightweight, low-energy models," Wil said under his breath.

"What's going on?" James98 demanded. "Where are you taking me? Ned? Whatever you're planning, reconsider."

"I'm done reconsidering things," Ned replied brusquely as he waddled back for the stairs with his limp load. "And I'd conserve power if I were you. Cal, here just severed every connection in your spine. Data, motor control, and, yes, power."

"Why?" James98 asked, as if the question were the last he might bother with as he clung to what little charge his skull kept locally.

Ned grunted. "Nothing personal. Just politics."

CHAPTER TWENTY-TWO

The alarm feature on Alan's portable was calibrated to his brainwaves. A school friend from his emancipation class had been working on it experimentally and had developed selective couples alarms. Kaylee's rarely woke Alan, and Alan's pretty much never disturbed Kaylee. A particular mixture of innocuous, rhythmic noises caught in his brain and broke his sleep pattern just long enough for him to wake up and shut off the sound.

He had a text message. It was Ned Lund.

GET DRESSED. MEET NOW. YOU'VE GOT 15 MINUTES
TO GET TO AIRLOCK 4.

Alan's heart raced.

A meter away, Kaylee snored.

The clock read 2:13 AM, Curiosity Standard Time.

This was it. They were bringing him in on something clandestine. His fingers shook as he searched the floor for the pants he'd discarded at bedtime. For once, his habit of ignoring the clothes processor was paying off.

Fully dressed in yesterday's attire, he tiptoed for the door before a pang of conscience stopped him short. Still creeping quietly through the bedroom, he leaned down and kissed Kaylee on the forehead.

She stirred and rolled onto her side.

"Honey, I have to go," Alan whispered, brushing aside a lock of hair that had fallen across her eye. With a groggy blink, that eye opened. "Spy stuff. Be back soon as I can."

"Be careful," Kaylee mumbled—or something close. It was hard to tell with her sleep-slurred speech.

Alan kissed her on the lips. She kissed back in a reflex honed over a decade and a half of marriage.

An instant later, he was gone.

The air in the common "outdoor" areas of the colony had never had that Earthy freshness to it. But he breathed deep of the microbially filtered air and felt free. A nervous jitter shook his shoulders. This was it. He was going to get a peek behind the curtain of the Martian resistance movement.

Airlock 4 wasn't far. But neither was fifteen minutes a long time. Alan referenced his portable on the way, checking to see when Ned had sent his message. Six minutes. He had nine left.

Alan set a brisk pace, wondering idly if there were hidden security camera monitoring the common areas. If he were to be fully inducted into the brotherhood of the Chain Breakers, he supposed he might have to learn that.

By the time he reached the airlock, Alan was breathing heavily. He hadn't quite jogged the kilometer or so from his apartment, but he wasn't exactly accustomed to long treks in such a short time frame.

Ned met him by the airlock door. "Got your breather?"

Alan blinked. "I, uh... don't have one."

Ned revealed a breather and goggles he'd been concealing behind his back. "Figured you'd forget. Here. And for future reference, you could have swiped your wife's. You'd have been back in plenty of time."

Kaylee's breather? It would sooner have occurred to him to borrow her underwear than her filtration mask. The former was just a frillier sort of undergarment. The latter was a lifesaving device she used every day of her professional life.

Ned's breather was already dangling around his neck. With a practiced tug and a flip, he had his on the instant the airlock door closed them in. Alan fumbled his borrowed set on, and Ned started the cycle.

Air rushed around them, exchanging colony air for the dead, wispy substance that passed for an atmosphere outside. Alan's ears popped. The outdoors was marginally lower pressure than inside. At least the terraforming efforts had gotten as far as building up the atmosphere's bulk if not its oxygen levels. Otherwise, they'd have needed full space suits to venture outside.

When the outer door opened, a bone-chilling wind greeted them. It was nighttime on Mars, and the greenhouse gasses weren't thick enough to trap the solar radiation from the daytime hours.

"Heavy coat, next time too," Ned warned, voice hollow behind his mask.

Alan nodded spasmodically, teeth already chattering.

It was warmer inside the rover. Alan didn't ask where they were headed but recognized their course from the previous visit to Mars Terraforming Initiative Site-2.

Questions boiled and churned in Alan's mind. He wanted to seem eager, willing, loyal to the cause. But this seemed like the kind of cause that preferred the back row students to the ones who sat up front and raised their hand at every question from the teacher.

Neither man spoke a word the whole drive out.

When the rover came to a halt, Alan and Ned got out and headed for the terraforming base camp's airlock. The process of exchanging Martian for science-cleansed air reversed, and the two of them trudged inside, stripping off their masks.

Luckily for Alan, the mask muffled his gasp of shock and horror.

"Who's that?" he dared to ask. There was a robot—Version 61 chassis if he wasn't mistaken—lying on the cafeteria table wearing a spacer's coveralls.

"James98," the robot said quietly. His optical sensors weren't even active. "Help me."

"Shaddup," Les said and slapped the robot across the face with a glove. He turned to Alan. "Don't mind him. He's just a prop. You're the guest of honor."

Alan whirled on Ned. The question must have been plain on his face because Ned answered without Alan having to say the words.

"Yeah," Ned said casually. "We figured we'd see what you're made of. Got a robot here who's not seeing the next Martian sunrise. Figured we'd allow you the privilege of getting a little revenge for all the wrongs robots have done you."

Alan backed toward the airlock door. "I... I..."

On the table, the robot sounded desperate. "I know Charlie7."

"So does every last one of you," Les snapped. "Can it, or I'll start drilling holes until I find the power supply to that voice modulator of yours."

"What did he do?" Alan asked in a tremulous voice.

"It's not so much what *he* did, it's what he's complicit in," Gregor explained. "Culpability is a shared commodity. Surely, James98 is a minor offender compared to some, but he *is* guilty of supporting the repressive regime on Earth."

Guilt. Complicity. Regime. This wasn't a committee meeting. This wasn't even a Human Era courtroom. This was a lynching for the robot era.

"This is murder," Alan protested.

"It's not a person," Ned assured him with a pat on the shoulder. "Must be hard, growing up on Earth. But you need to understand, it's just a machine programmed to think like one. They stole minds and mushed them together into a working model of a human brain. But it hasn't got real feelings. It hasn't got a soul. You a religious fellow, Alan?"

Alan nodded mutely. He wasn't the scientist that Kaylee was, but neither of them had the first inkling of how the known cosmos came to be. Consciousness was an inexplicable phenomenon, replicable by roboticists but never understood fully. Alan had to believe that there was some greater force in the universe that had gifted it to mankind and through them, to robots.

And there was a consciousness trapped in that metallic skull. The limp chassis, helpless on the table, wouldn't respond to its owner's commands. James98 had been forbidden to speak on pain of involuntary modification. Robots didn't feel pain as such, but they could receive dire error messages, and they could certainly experience terror.

Alan could imagine nothing so horrifying as being trapped in his own mind, able—no, compelled—to listen in as a cabal of murderers spoke glibly of the reasons to annihilate his consciousness.

Ned pressed a device into Alan's hand. "Go on, then. Do it. If you don't, one of us will. There's no saving this one."

Looking down, Alan saw a magnetic device, some sort of alignment tool or calibrator. Kaylee would know its proper function. All Alan saw, however, was a murder weapon.

"Just hold it to the skull—mind your fingers, of course—and hit the button on the side," Les explained, pointing to a spot on the side of James98's cranium. "Clickity-clack. No more robot."

"Don't worry," Wil said. "If you're worried about getting caught, don't be. We've blanked transorbital crew before. A little repair work and it'll look just like a suicide. Every few trips, one of those ships comes back with a blank chassis or two."

"They send 'em back on autopilot," Calvin added. "Don't sweat it. We'll do the heavy lifting dragging this one back."

"Please," James98 moaned.

"Aww, forget it," Les snapped testily. "This one's got no 'sterone." He snatched the magnetic device from Alan's hand and applied it to James98's head.

"No!" Alan shouted and lunged for the device.

Ned caught him by the arms and held him back. There was a clack and a thunk. Ned released Alan then, but it was already too late.

"Why?" Alan pleaded. The time for playing along had expired. So had Alan's chances of escape. Ned was between him and the airlock, and even his most optimistic assessment informed him that he'd never get past the solidly built terraformer.

Les shook his head in disappointment. "It's them or us, kid. But you don't get it. Or if you do, you don't have the stomach to do anything about it."

"Either way, you've become a liability," Ned said.

Alan's bladder clenched. He'd never pissed himself before, but his nether regions were giving the matter hasty consideration. "You can't. They'll look for me. They'll investigate. Kaylee's got connections!" A note of panic crept in as his would-be captors remained impassive.

"See?" Wil said to Ned. "The Earthlings always go crony when it gets tough. Can't just admit they're on their own on the red planet."

"You'll never get away with this!" Alan promised, backing against the wall of the break room.

"Us?" Ned asked incredulously. "Why would we get away with anything?"

They came at him as a group. Hands grabbed. Bodies pressed. Alan thrashed, but his efforts were ineffectual. Ned and his cronies dragged him over to the deceased James98. Someone pulled his arm outstretched. Alan couldn't see what they were doing. They forced his fingers spread.

Fire.

Pain.

Burning.

Just a cut, but a ragged one, he saw as they released him.

"You're the one who killed this poor, defenseless robot," Ned said. With a hand, he showed Alan how they'd cut his finger on a ragged edge where they'd severed James98's spine. "You might want to get that tended to quietly. Looks mighty suspicious."

The terraformers didn't allow him time to staunch the bleeding. As he kept it covered by the sleeve of his shirt, they forced on his filtration mask and goggles. Dragging him out the airlock with them, the five of them piled into the rover with the inert robot wrapped in a tarp.

His mind a maelstrom of emotions, Alan tried to board the vehicle along with them. His only thoughts consisted of getting back home and tending to his injured hand. Surely, they weren't going to let him die out there.

But the rover door closed. Alan circled to the opposite side, but Les gave him a shove that sent him sprawling to the red rock planetary surface.

As he watched the rover depart, Alan knew that he was in trouble. Even if they had left the base unlocked, going back in would no doubt play into their hands. They had to have put a contingency together for that.

Tucking his maimed hand under his arm, he fiddled with his goggles until he found the retractable data cable. Plugging the end into a port on his breather, a display popped up in the corner of his field of vision.

He had fifty-eight minutes of oxygen left.

There was no time for math. He set a course for the Airlock-4 and prayed that Ned hadn't locked him out there too.

CHAPTER TWENTY-THREE

Kaylee rolled over and shut off her alarm. She rolled the other way to give Alan a kiss before starting her day. She often headed off to work before he even roused himself from bed, so it wasn't unusual for her to—

He was gone.

The apartment was quiet.

Kaylee wracked her brain. Something was missing, more than just her husband. A memory tickled, half-formed, at the back of her brain. He'd gone off in the middle of the night. She'd dismissed it as a dream. Now, as she checked the kitchen, living room, and bathroom of the tiny apartment, evidence was mounting that it hadn't been.

She checked her portable for messages. Nothing from Alan. The only text that had come in was from Ned, telling her to report to Site-2 that morning. He'd gotten an inside scoop that Earth was pulling strings and might manage to divert enough steel their way to resume construction.

Kaylee wasn't going anywhere until she found Alan.

Her first step was the obvious. She texted him a quick, "Miss you. Where are you?" Nothing alarmist. Nothing incriminating. He probably *had* told her where he was heading in the dead of night, and she'd just forgotten. The last thing she needed was to ask about his secret assignment while a bunch of Chain Breakers were standing around to see over his shoulder.

Still, how long had he been gone? Alan wasn't good in social situations to begin with. He got sweaty-palmed and antsy at birthday parties if they dragged on too long. How could he bear the company of those Neanderthal freaks and their bigoted jokes?

She waited by the portable, leaving it on the kitchen table open to the chat program. Mind elsewhere, she sleepwalked through the process of making an oatmeal breakfast.

The apartment door opened.

Alan stumbled inside with a grunt of relief. One arm was tucked against his chest, his hand wedged beneath his other arm.

"Alan!" Kaylee shouted, not caring whether the neighbors heard through the walls. "What happened to you?"

Rushing to his side, she wanted to wrap her arms around him but thought better of it. Instead, she took him by the shoulders and looked into his eyes.

"I'm fine," he said, but there was no life in his voice. He shuffled past Kaylee, not quite pushing her out of his way but not waiting for her to clear a path either.

Kaylee trailed him toward the bathroom. "Where have you been? What did you get mixed up in?"

"Later," Alan said. "Just... give me a minute."

The door closed, separating them. The sink ran. Clothes fell to the floor. Alan grunted and groaned softly. A crinkling sounded like a med kit's contents.

"If I don't get answers, I'm coming in there to inspect you myself," Kaylee threatened through the door.

"Long night. Need shower." True to his word, the shower started seconds later. The rushing waterfall of droplets pelting the shower floor cut off as Alan stepped in to block the flow with his body.

Kaylee had taken this long enough.

The bathroom door was locked, but it was a residential model. The lock was privacy only. Kaylee punched in the emergency responders' code and let herself inside.

"Hey!" Alan yelped. It was the most animated he'd been since arriving back from his mystery errand.

Alan's clothes were caked in red-tinged dust. A self-sealing bandage lay discarded at the edge of the sink, smeared with blood. There was a tinge of blood at the edges of the sink as well, where the puddle of water filled as the spout and drain reached equilibrium.

"Get out," Alan groused. "I'll explain when I get out."

That wasn't good enough. Kaylee was only wearing her nightgown. She untied the drawstring and let it fall beside Alan's planet-stained attire. With a quick tug of the curtain, she joined him in the shower.

"You're going to tell me what's going on. *Now*," Kaylee insisted. She took him by the wrist and raised Alan's freshly bandaged hand. "Starting with this."

Alan turned, letting the water from the showerhead splatter down his back and matte his hair against his head. "They're going to try to frame me. I don't know what to do yet. All I know is that I've got to be bright-eyed and bushy-tailed at the school by 9:00 sharp and have an explanation for this hand injury that'll stand up to the inquiries of a bunch of conniving teenagers."

"What *did* happen to your hand?" Kaylee asked, pleading for details that Alan was shying from like the edge of a cliff.

"They killed a robot, Kay," Alan said. The look in his eyes as he shook his head in disbelief was haunted. "James98. Did you know him?"

Kaylee shook her head.

"He was on the transorbital that docked yesterday, dropping off ice for the melting fields. They ambushed him, cut his spine. I don't know how they got the jump on him. But they wanted me to blank him. I had the EMP right in my hand."

"You didn't..."

Alan shook his head, wincing in a sure sign of a headache. "Of course, not! You know me. But that was it for my ruse of fitting in. They suspected me. It was a test. I failed."

"So they did this to your hand?" Kaylee asked, trying to make sense of it all. The punishment seemed ill fit to the crime, from the Chain Breakers' perspective. Alan was still a witness, and the hand injury didn't look *too* severe. Was it supposed to be a preview of injuries to come if he turned them in?

"Worse," Alan said. "They made it look like I'd cut it on James98's chassis. Not only do I now look like a murderer once the chassis is discovered, I look like a clumsy one."

"Turn them in!" Kaylee insisted, blinking away the droplets that splashed in her eyes. "This is a win."

"They've had an hour's head start on me," Alan said. "They'll have dummied up the evidence. It'll be five against one. They know the colony's security and systems. My only chance is to go along with the cover-up."

Kaylee shook her head. "No. We can't let them win."

"It's a war. We lost a battle tonight," Alan said. "This is more than a single event. Even if Ned and the others get caught, if Earth punishes them for the crime, it'll just sow more discontent. We need to pull the Chain Breakers up by the roots."

"It's not fair," Kaylee said, slumping against Alan's bare, wet chest. "You got them. You caught them red-handed."

Alan pulled her against him, shielding her from the hot water that steamed the air enclosed with them. She could feel the slick smoothness of the bandage on his injured hand, a reminder that their safety was a tenuous blessing. "Don't go to work today."

In the tight quarters, Kaylee could only shake her head a twitch. "I have to. We're restarting work on Site-2, banking on the committees wrangling us some materials to get construction moving. I have to be there. Ned will be suspicious. You didn't tell him I knew, did you?"

"No," Alan said, "but that doesn't mean he won't assume. It's too risky."

"We came here to make a home," Kaylee reminded him. "Ned might be a bad apple, but the project is still a key to Mars as a living planet. I don't want to live under a dome the rest of my life."

"Just today..." Alan pleaded.

Kaylee put a finger to his lips. "Especially today. We can't let them bully us into a life of fear. Besides, they need me. Without me, Site-1 was a Sisyphean nightmare of false starts and rebuilds. It's either keep me around or let robots onto the project."

Alan pulled the rest of her hand to his lips and kissed it. "We both know they need you. But I need you more."

Kaylee stared deep into her husband's eyes. There was a difference between following a wife on her Martian adventure and joining a political movement. He'd endangered himself to safeguard her dream for an idyllic colonial life. It was seeing that fire, a hot ember that couldn't be doused by even the prospect of being framed for murder. Her lips covered his. Her tongue pushed past.

As she reached down and pulled Alan's hips against hers, he suddenly pulled back. "Temperature, 10 degrees."

Kaylee gasped at the shock of cold water suddenly drenching them both. She pressed against Alan's body not with the passionate urgency of a moment earlier. Now, it was for simple warmth.

"Shut it off! Shut it off!" But Alan had started the shower. It was keyed to his voice for the duration—ironically, a safeguard against just the sort of prank he had just played.

"Temperature, 40 degrees," Alan said.

The shower water resumed its soothing warmth.

"What was that for?" Kaylee demanded disappointedly. These last days since joining up with the Unity Keepers had rekindled a desire for Alan that she'd rarely felt since their honeymoon. She pillowed her head on his shoulder.

"We both have work today. We don't have time."

"Plenty of time," Kaylee muttered, giving her husband a playful slap on the backside as she exited the shower in search of a towel. She missed her cyclonic drying chamber from their Paris home. She left her words purposefully muddy as she added in an undertone just loud enough to hear, "high opinion of himself."

She and Alan got dressed side by side. Neither of them had properly cleaned under the water, but Alan had been right. Both of them needed to get moving, or they'd be late.

When they parted ways at the door after a kiss, Alan waved a goodbye. The sight of the bandage on his hand scraped aside the veneer of normalcy their daily routine had tried to paint over the dangers they faced.

But Alan was going to school. Kaylee was the one headed for Airlock 4 to join Ned's prep team at Site-2.

CHAPTER TWENTY-FOUR

Kaylee needed a painstaking, technical, exacting installation, alignment, or calibration to keep her mind too busy to worry what Ned and his thugs had done to Alan last night—and what they might have in store next. A day with an engrossing task could pass in the blink of an eye. She desperately needed that today.

Instead, of course, Kaylee was assigned a micro-scrubber and sent off to clean oxidized deposits from the intake manifolds of the Site-2 atmospheric purifier. It was drone work—or would have been on Earth. Mars was short both the drones and drone programmers needed to be using them on minor, one-off tasks like site prep. The majority of the colony's drones would be working on unloading the transorbital's payload and dragging ice chunks ranging in side from a thumbnail to a skyro out into the melting fields. It was all automated. None of the drones would question where James98 had gone or why he hadn't been back. His own crew mates probably hadn't even noticed. Robots mining that far out were notoriously antisocial. They'd let the drones do their job and head right back out to the belt for more.

Bloody Earthlings and their monopoly on drone production, she caught herself thinking. If only Mars had a Kanto-style factory. Even on a vastly smaller scale, it could help them automate manual labor across the colonies.

Listen to yourself. Already siding with the enemy.

Whatever Ned and his Chain Breaker cronies' political views were, they crossed the line into zealotry the minute they devolved into violence. Robots used the nice, sterile term "self-termination" for suicide, but murder was still murder whether it was James98 or a human victim.

Bundled against the outdoor chill and wearing goggles and oxygen supplies, she and her coworkers looked like walking parkas with data-screen eyes. They could have been robots beneath all that layered cloth, except that an actual robot wouldn't have minded the cold or needed breathing assistance.

There wasn't even a clock in view as Kaylee worked.

All the other supervisors and managers were out there as well, toiling away with their practiced and highly skilled hands at work best suited to burly day-laborers, if not robots. Kaylee wasn't the only one whose talents were being wasted; she had no right to complain. If nothing else, the isolation as everyone huddled in their own personal refuge of warm clothing prevented just the sort of awkward interaction she'd so desperately wished to avoid today.

As she scrubbed, she watched them.

It was hard to pick out one coworker from the next. Their mass-fabbed parkas were identical. Their protective environmental gear was all from the same design, manufactured over at the Discovery colony a few hundred kilometers to the east. At best, she could judge by mannerisms. A distinctive walk, a limp, a rounded shoulder were her clues.

Ned she picked out early and kept close track of.

Alan, I hope your day is going better than mine, she pleaded silently.

Kaylee kept her portable handy in her pocket. If one of the workers looked ready to sabotage the manifold or any other part of the terraforming equipment, she'd be ready to capture it on video.

But none of them were so sloppy as to get caught on her watch.

When she'd first worried about saboteurs, she'd dismissed the idea as fanciful and paranoid. Ned wanted Mars to breathe Martian air instead of recycled. He wanted to stick it to Earth worse than anyone she'd ever known. Hurting that goal would be the last thing on his mind.

Until she thought deeper on the subject.

Yes, Ned might delay the work on a single site by having someone sabotage it. But if he could connect the damage back to Earth sympathizers, or better—from his viewpoint—a robot, then he could use that persecution to strong-arm his way past committee roadblocks with sympathy as his bludgeon. Anyone who stood in his way then would be complicit with the saboteurs.

Knowing what she now knew thanks to Alan's predicament, Kaylee was convinced that Ned had the deviousness to think that far ahead and delay his own immediate gratification for a longer-term win.

Alan... poor Alan. He meant so well, but he stumbled right into that trap. If she'd been awake enough to talk sense into him, he might not be lined up in the crosshairs of a frame job. Kaylee prayed that James98 had been the depressive sort so that no one would look too deeply into his apparent self-termination. Knowing that Ned could plunk Alan into the witness chair at a committee inquest on a whim was going to cost her many a sleepless night, she knew.

"Kaylee, c'mon in," Ned's voice grated in her earpiece. "Lunch break."

Kaylee felt the knot of hunger in her stomach, exacerbated by skipping breakfast in her haste to make up for a slapdash morning. "I'm good," she radioed back. She watched as her coworkers filed into the break room airlock. "Had a big breakfast, knowing we had real work to do for a change."

"Suit yourself," came the gruff reply.

As soon as the last of the terraforming team was inside, Kaylee pulled out her portable. With a glove off her right hand to operate the touch screen, she felt the crisp bite of the thin atmosphere. She and Alan had spent a week in Mexico City to acclimate to the low pressure, but it still hadn't compared to being on the Martian surface.

She tapped out a message with a hand shaking from the cold.

"What did you get him into?" Kaylee sent the message off to Andy. It was nice and generic. No names. No specific events. She wondered what he could feel safe replying.

NO NEWS. COME BACK AFTER WORK.

Kaylee seethed a frustrated breath that made her next breath humid inside the mask. Alan hadn't reported in. Andy was blind to what was going on. One of them had to get him a briefing.

She resolved to head over to the theater after work, but in the meantime, she tapped out another message.

"Alan was accosted by the Chain Breakers last night. If I'm not around to deliver this message, it's because one of them got to me. James98 was murdered by Ned Lund and his associates. They cut Alan's hand on the chassis in order to frame him. Don't let them sweep this under the rug."

She set the delivery to tomorrow afternoon, then buried the outgoing message in an archival directory. A real data wrangler would find it with no trouble, sent or not, but a casual inspection from the likes of Ned and his gang wouldn't find anything.

Slipping her glove back on, Kaylee returned to her task.

Post lunch, the terraforming crew resumed reconditioning machinery left idle and unattended for months longer than expected. Kaylee finished up on her section of the intake manifold and moved on to the waste pumps. Despite the layer of rust, they were still cleaner than they'd ever be once operation got under way.

By the end of the shift, Kaylee felt like she'd been at the job site for a year, not a mere ten hours.

The crew rode back to Airlock 4 in a convoy of rovers and parted ways once they were back inside the dome.

Mask dangling around her neck, Kaylee headed straight for Arthur Miller Theater.

"There you are!" Andy said accusingly. He towed her from the common area where several other Unity Keepers were idling after work and down an adjacent hall lined with dressing rooms. An old-fashioned swinging door slammed shut behind them. "What the blazes is going on? Back channel, I heard the Breakers took Alan out for some kind of initiation last night."

"You tell me," Kaylee said. "This is your secret agent act that got his cover blown. They know he was a plant."

"Oh, God!" Andy said, covering his mouth. He dove for his portable. "I need to—"

Kaylee caught him by the wrist. "He's fine. Alan went to class this morning, same as usual."

Andy had a haunted look in his eyes. "We haven't had anyone outed before. This is bad."

"No kidding," Kaylee said. "We need a plan."

"I need the details. Are you *sure* Alan is OK?"

"I checked with the school on the way over. He's busy with after-school tutoring. Safest place in the colony, if you ask me. *Nobody* wants to be the one to endanger kids."

At Andy's urging, Kaylee recounted Alan's tale as best she could remember it. Andy listened attentively without interruption.

"Who else have you told?" Andy asked.

"No one," Kaylee replied. "You're the first besides Alan, and I don't think *he* was inclined to spread the word."

"No... no, that wouldn't make sense," Andy said as he began to pace, not even looking in Kaylee's direction. "Not in such a precarious predicament. One wrong word in the wrong ear..."

"I did compose a message to go out tomorrow in case I didn't make it here," Kaylee said, taking out her portable and waggling it.

"To whom?" Andy asked.

"You, mainly."

"And...?" he prompted.

Kaylee was horrible at lies and secrets. She couldn't have left it at just Andy. "Possibly my mom, a couple aunts, Dr. Toby, my mother-in-law, and maybe my great-grandmother."

"You were going to alert half of Earth's most prominent humans and an original thirty-three robot about a suspicious murder that implicates your husband?"

Kaylee sighed. "*And* Charlie7."

Andy looked aghast.

"He's an old family friend. I trust him."

Kaylee wondered if this was what it was like for the people in those old Mafia movies, totally innocent of the greater family business but still aware that certain problems could go away by dropping the right word of complaint at Thanksgiving dinner.

"Delete it," Andy ordered sternly, the first thing he'd seemed certain of since her arrival.

"We need to put a stop to whatever they're doing to Alan," Kaylee said. "Even if that means covering up the death of James98 until we can prove it was them."

The door to the dressing room burst open, splinters flew where the doorjamb gave way under the force of a booted foot. Wil from the terraforming team backed out of the doorway to allow Ned Lund inside.

"About time we found out where you rats were hiding," Ned said to Andy. He looked the theater director up and down. "Never imagined it would be a wet noodle like you playing rebel."

"Just like I said," Gregor Zimmerman said calmly. "Let her go. She'll lead us right to them. Who needs the teacher?"

"What's this about, Ned?" Kaylee demanded. "You just go barging into a dressing room. What if I'd been—"

"Cut the crap," Ned barked. His cronies filed in, greater in numbers than Kaylee had imagined. "We know who you people are and what you've been trying to do. You've been enemies of Mars for too long. It's about time we put you to work on our side."

Kaylee and Andy were hauled out of the dressing room, feet not even touching the floor. In the main backstage area, the rest of the Unity Keepers who'd been present had already been rounded up and penned in by armed Chain Breakers.

"What are those collars for?" Andy asked.

Kaylee saw what he was referring to. The others had all been fitted with makeshift collars fashioned from piping meant for use as electrical conduit. Each had a small indicator panel with a glowing red light at the center.

She struggled as two of Ned's goons forced one around her own neck with an ominous click. Ned held up a remote. "Those are insurance. They'll blow your head right off if you get more than a few meters away or I press this button.

"Now sit down, shut up, and don't cause any trouble. I've got a broadcast to make."

Before forcing Kaylee to the floor, the Chain Breakers confiscated Kaylee's portable. Even with an exploding collar freshly locked at her throat, all she could think about was the emergency message contained on it. What would they do to her if they discovered she was sending distress calls to the primary villains of their conspiracy theories?

CHAPTER TWENTY-FIVE

lan sat in the office behind his classroom, trying to appear relaxed in the Earth-made wooden chair he'd brought with him from Oxford. His portable was on silent mode, tucked away in a drawer.

He'd spent the past half hour trying to explain why the fall of the Roman Empire at the hands of Germanic tribes was not the end of civilization for the next eight hundred years until the Renaissance.

Alan gestured with his hand to emphasize his point. "There was a local decline in the standard of living, yes, but—"

"They didn't reinvent concrete for another fifteen hundred years," Tina Lobson argued. "It's just one example, but the average Roman citizen lived better than a twelfth-century king."

"Debatable," Alan allowed. "But you're still overlooking the wider world. During that same time, the Chinese Dynasties carried on as if nothing had happened—for them, nothing of consequence had. Movable type, the compass, and the mechanical clock all came from China during the European Dark Ages."

"Gutenberg invented movable type," Tina argued smugly.

Alan forced his jaw to unclench before replying. "He invented a mechanical press. A man named Bi Sheng invented movable block type during the Song Dynasty four hundred years before that."

Tina scowled at him.

"Look it up on the Solarwide when you get home. I want you to write up a five-page research paper on advancements during the Dark Ages that took place in Asia, Africa, and the Middle East."

Tina got up and collected her school bag. "Stupid Earth history," he heard her mutter on the way out the door.

Alan didn't care about the slight just then. Tina had been the last of his after-school appointments. He slouched in his chair and dug through his desk drawer to pull out his portable.

No one had asked about his hand. The antiseptic and anesthetic properties of the self-adhesive bandage had kept the wound from bothering him beyond a simple reduction in mobility. He'd made it to the end of the day relatively unscathed.

Pressing a thumb against the screen to unlock the device, he swiped through his message box. He'd arranged so that anything from Kaylee or Andy would get swamped in a morass of idle chatter from old colleagues on Earth, emancipation classmates he'd kept in touch with over the years, and committee summaries he got automatically delivered from topics of interest. He didn't want any message previews to be seen by young, curious eyes.

WHERE ARE YOU?

EVERYTHING OK?

MEET FOR LUNCH?

CATCH YOU AFTER WORK?

CALLED THE SCHOOL. KNOW YOU'RE TUTORING. TEXT AND I'LL START DINNER. SEE YOU AT HOME.

All from Kaylee. Sent at intervals throughout the day. A pang of guilt stabbed him in the gut with the worry he'd obviously caused her. He tapped out a quick message back in reply to the final missive.

"Be home soon. Love you."

Alan packed up and closed the office door behind him. The vacant classroom was peaceful and silent, a hermit crab's shell waiting for students to come back and inhabit it.

A chime rang from his portable as he closed up the classroom. "What the—I've had that off all day."

This message had an override. Emergency broadcast, civic-wide for the Curiosity colony.

"*Breaking news. Hostage standoff at Arthur Miller Theater. Masked individuals are holding eight human hostages. Details are still coming in. Colony Mayor Dana Platt warns citizens to keep clear of the area while emergency response personnel negotiate for the safe release of the—Wait... we have a video clip released by the hostage takers. You are receiving this broadcast live as it is released.*"

Alan walked in a daze, eyes fixed on his portable.

The man in the goggles and breather mask was Ned—there was no mistaking him, and his identity wouldn't remain secret long.

Dread sank in as Ned read off a list of demands. But the words dripped out Alan's ears unheard.

In the background of the video, he saw her. Kaylee. Wearing some kind of collar. Oh, God, Alan had gotten Kaylee taken as a hostage! He should never have agreed to spy for that rotten bastard, Andy. Kaylee would have been safe if Alan hadn't tried to play the hero and gotten cold feet when it came to murdering an already-doomed robot. *He* might not have been a murderer, but Ned Lund most certainly was. There was no time to lose.

Alan blundered into a doorway in his haste to exit the school, dropping his portable and not pausing to retrieve it. Pelting down the streets of Curiosity, heedless of the colonists wandering in the direction of the spectacle, Alan discarded his school rucksack in his haste to get to Arthur Miller Theater.

Curiosity colony wasn't huge. In five minutes, he'd made his way to the humble, four-story structure. A drone was planting parade-route markers as an interim cordon to designate the official exclusion zone. A handful of city officials gathered in a knot, huddled in conversation just behind the plastic ribbon strung between weighted posts.

As Alan dashed for the cordon, one of the officials perked up. "Sir, you can't go—"

"My wife is in there!" Alan shouted back. He tried to vault the ribbon but caught a foot and crashed to the concrete pavement, knocking over two of the support posts. As the drone circled back to right them, Alan scrambled to his feet and continued into the building before anyone could stop him.

He burst through the front door. "Kaylee! Where are—?"

A heavy blow caught Alan on the side of the head before he even saw who was on the other side of the main door. He was out cold before he hit the floor.

CHAPTER TWENTY-SIX

C harlie7 kept an informal record ranking his good and bad days. Over his lifespan of more than eleven hundred years, it was an impressive list. It scaled from zero to one hundred, calibrated with the day he discovered the last human had died in the alien invasion as a rank of zero and the day he launched an interplanetary projectile to (presumably) destroy their homeworld as a rank of one hundred.

The day he'd discovered Eve14, the first healthy, mentally competent human of the new era, had rated ninety-nine. Finding out that political dissidents on Mars had taken hostages had pegged today for an eight. Discovering that Eve's great granddaughter and Dr. Toby's youngest son were among the hostages dropped it to a four with room to drop should things get worse.

Charlie7 stormed into the meeting chamber of the Human Welfare Committee ready to receive word of a military action to retrieve the victims.

Instead, he found the committee in session, debating the merits of incarceration versus exile for the hostage takers.

"I don't see how social isolation benefits us *or* them, long term," Ruby Barton said. "This is all an educational failure. All violent ends are a result of communication breakdowns, and in this case, it appears to have been allowed to fester uncorrected for far too long. First a riot targeting a robot. Now, emboldened by our inaction, they've taken human hostages."

Another of the committee members rose to speak, but Eve tapped a finger on the glossy surface of the table. Speakers in the room projected the sound of a gavel banging with each tap.

"The chair recognizes Charlie7, come to give us the latest on the tactical situation," Eve said deliberately.

Charlie7 marched up to the spot where guest speakers normally addressed the committee and kept on walking. He didn't stop until he was looming over the head of poor Nathan Spence, right at the voting members' table. "It's grim. The hostages are all wearing collars of homemade design. Ned Lund is acting as spokesman for the hostage takers, and he claims they're rigged with explosives. If we try to free the hostages or attack any of the hostage takers, they'll—"

Jennifer81 raised a hand to forestall gory details. "We can fill in the blanks."

"The devices are primitive. We can't hack our way in to disarm them," Charlie7 continued. "It may even be possible that they're entirely analog."

"Has anyone confirmed the identities of the hostages?" Ruby asked.

"By process of elimination, Curiosity colonial authorities have narrowed down who is in Arthur Miller Theater. We've visually confirmed some on camera, but we can't be 100 percent certain who's a hostage and who's a hostage taker. Not conclusively. From Social use, however, we've got a pretty damn good idea. Eight hostage takers. A dozen hostages, even. They haven't set a timetable for their demands yet, but somewhere, in the head of one of those Neddites, is a ticking clock."

"We'd be lucky if there's that much in there," Eve said with gallows humor.

"Neddites?" Jennifer81 asked. "The news feeds are calling them Chain Breakers."

"They don't get to give themselves an aggrandizing name on my watch," Charlie7 said. "Any press releases from our end will refer to them as Neddites. That Lund character wants to put his neck on the line, we'll hang this movement on him."

A tentative hand raised from the table. Serena Jones asked, "Can you list their demands? I haven't been able to bring myself to watch the video."

Inwardly, Charlie7 rolled his eyes. There was one who didn't belong in a position of this magnitude. Doing right by the welfare of humankind meant facing the evils of society head on. If those evils went without rearing their ugly heads for decades at a time, all the better, but when the time came, limp dishcloths like Serena Jones had to be ready to take a stand and do the job they'd wheeled their way into.

"Ned Lund has set a series of demands for the release of the hostages," Charlie7 said. "He has promised no releases until all demands are met. He wants the following: the return of the Truman-Effect reactor originally designated for Curiosity Terraforming Site-2, a laundry list of processed ores, the repatriation of all Martian-born children attending Oxford, five seats on the Human Welfare Committee to be voted on and filled by Martian natives, and Martian control of two asteroid mining vessels."

"Why doesn't he ask for his own private colony dome on Phobos while he's at it," Eve said bitterly. "He knows we can't deliver all that."

"We could," Charlie7 said with a shrug. "We *have* all that on Earth."

"We don't bargain with terrorists," Eve stated firmly.

Again, Charlie7 shrugged. "An old doctrine, dredged up from the archives."

Eve's chest heaved. "This is an outrage! I will *not* buy back stolen lives at the profit of the thieves. I want better options, Charlie. Give me something better."

"There are three tried-and-true methods," Charlie7 said easily. Allowing Eve her righteous anger permitted him to ignore his own for the moment. "We can bait-and-switch them... promise the moon and stars but deliver a hoax."

"Keep trying," Eve muttered, wheezing with each breath.

"We could stage an assault. Hit them hard and fast, maybe gradually introduce a breathable sedative to the air to dull their reactions. Maybe we disable them in time to stop the Neddites from detonating the bomb collars. Risky but decisive. We'd have to accept a high probability of casualties, potentially up to 100 percent."

"Go... on... still not..." Eve said, gasping for breath now.

Charlie7 burst into motion, scattering bystanders and sending committee members diving onto the table to get out of his way. He was just in time to catch Eve as she toppled over the side of her chair, struggling to breathe.

"Get a doctor in here!" Charlie7 shouted. The stress had gotten to her. Veins normally filled with engine coolant weren't running so cold as they used to. Teetering on the brink of collapse to begin with, Charlie7's casual talk of the potential death of her great granddaughter—and genetic twin—had been too much.

As the emergency medical staff swooped in, Charlie7 backed off and let them work. He didn't have time to explain the final option, the one with the best chance of a favorable outcome: send in a negotiator.

But now, mankind's greatest and most influential voice was sidelined. As Eve was whisked off to nearby Franklin Hospital, he wondered who could fill that enormous void.

CHAPTER TWENTY-SEVEN

The acoustics of Notre Dame were simply divine. The robots attending services had no ear for music. They could replicate the sounds of song but some element of passion was lost along the way. Abby Fourteen sat among them, one of just a handful of humans mixed in among the pews.

She sat near the back. Her voice was quiet and weak but still well trained. Range and volume eluded her, but she still had an ear to measure her harmony as she accompanied the surrounding robots in their hymns. She'd liked to hear another 127-year-old sing so well.

All too soon, the hymns ended. There were readings and blessings and rituals of all manner that followed, but Abby's mind wandered. She had read and memorized so many literary works of the Human Age in an effort to evoke the souls of her forbearers in her songs and plays. Among those esteemed works were every major holy book, and she'd learned to read eleven languages in order to experience as many as possible in their original tongue. The Old and New Testaments she had read in Hebrew, Greek, and Latin, in addition to canonical English translations. Every word John316 spoke in front of the altar, Abby knew by rote.

When it came time for communion, Abby kept to her seat. Keeping her eyes respectfully downcast, she waited while the congregation took their share of the wafers and wine—even the robots. Abby didn't pretend to understand the metaphysics at work there.

Patience was a virtue that came easily to the aged, and Abby was no exception. Before too long had passed, John316 bid his flock a final, "Go in peace."

"Thanks be to God," the congregation replied before dispersing to the exits.

Abby kept her seat.

When the cathedral had cleared, Abby made her way to the confessionals and took a seat inside. It was dark and cozy with a musty scent of incense and wood polish evoking the Human Era. Few places on Earth could transport her back there so vividly.

After a moment, the door to the other side of the confessional opened, and John316 sat down across the wooden screen partition from her. "How long has it been since your last confession?"

Abby scowled for a moment. "Bless me, Father, for I have sinned. It has been 8,572 days since my last confession. On the whole, I think I've been pretty well behaved in the meantime. All the sins of not going to church, sure... maybe more than a fair share of pride. But that's not why I'm here."

"It might do you good to unburden your soul," John316 suggested, as mild a rebuke as Abby could recall receiving.

"I'm really thinking that confession was a one-time affair for me. What I'm really looking for is insight into a mass existential crisis on Mars," Abby said.

"Indeed."

"I need to understand... well, *you*," Abby said. "Every year, it seems, I get a new organ replaced by cybernetics. Ten years back, it was my knees. Twenty back, it was my eyes—and I wish now I'd gotten them swapped out when I was seventy. I've had one piece of me or another mechanical since I was in my twenties. But no one has ever suggested that I don't have a soul."

"And you're questioning exactly when that separation might take place?" John316 asked. "My dear, there is no medical procedure that can excise the soul from the body. So long as you live, it resides within you."

"And robots," Abby said. "How or why do you have a soul?"

John316 sighed. "Despite our detractors, I believe that God imbues every robot with an immortal soul at upload. Each creature that evolved upon the Earth was new at some point and, great and small, He has graced us."

"What about going the other direction?" Abby asked. "Gemini, for example?"

"I would not speculate on the grace of that one's soul," John316 said primly. "But, strictly theologically speaking, she ought to have kept her soul at upload."

"What about the robotic copy that still believed it was Evelyn11?" Abby pressed.

"I don't see how this relates to your initial claim that this was about a spiritual crisis on Mars."

That was as good as admitting he didn't know, in Abby's book. There was a whir of servos as she put a hand to the screen. "There's a temporal crisis on Mars right now."

"I am aware of the regrettable incident," John316 stated. "I will be praying for a safe resolution."

An alarm chimed in Abby's ear—a reminder.

"Thanks," Abby said, though the robotic priest hadn't been much help. "I've got to go."

"Are you sure you're well?" John316 asked. "Spiritual conundrums often crop up when one is feeling their mortality creep in."

"Me and my mortality aren't on speaking terms," Abby replied brusquely. "Any time it rears its ugly head, I replace whatever's broken. I've just got to get home. I'm expecting company."

CHAPTER TWENTY-EIGHT

Charlie7 found himself, more and more, the bearer of bad news. It was a peculiar burden he carried, willing to shoulder the unpleasantness of conversations that robots and humans alike shied from, all because he'd seen and been through so much worse.

No one had a zero day as bad as Charlie7's.

Today's onerous errand drew him back to the shadow of his own home beneath the Arc de Triomphe. Paris had taken its global prominence in the Second Human Age thanks to his residence there. A shy, tentative Eve had made it her home to lean on him for advice and protection—better protection than Plato gave her, despite his best intentions.

But others had settled in the city as well. Phoebe had made it her life's work to breathe life into the wildflower fields that had overgrown the grand old Roman city of Lutetia. Titus Labienus had conquered it from savage tribes. Saint Denis had died on that hill over yonder. Joan of Arc, Louis XIV, Robespierre, Napoleon, and Charles de Gaulle had all walked these lands.

It had been a shame to see them reclaimed by uncaring nature.

It was one of the oldest residents in the city that was the target of today's errand. Only Charlie7 himself, a scattering of robots, and her own mother could lay claim to more years than Abbigail Fourteen among the locals.

Charlie7 hated disturbing her.

At some point, humans crossed a threshold between hale vigor and clinging to the driftwood of a sinking life. Eve was closer to her end than Charlie7 cared to admit. The old bird knew it, too, and fought back every step of the way, plodding forward with her official duties as the Grim Reaper stubbornly clung to her ankles, wishing he'd gone into some other line of work. The humans of the Second Human Era were a resilient lot.

Eve and Plato had been young—in the early blossoming of that hale stretch of life—when they'd adopted her. In relative terms, Abby wasn't *that* much younger. However, at the moment, what Charlie7 needed was a Madison genome body with a few extra years less wear-and-tear. If he couldn't present the hostage takers with Eve, at least he had the next best thing.

He left his skyroamer parked in front of the house, strode up to the front door, and rang the chime. "Abby, it's me, Charlie7, I—"

The voice came through the door-side speaker. *"Just a minute. I'm almost done."*

Charlie7 pressed the chime again. It wouldn't alert Abby again so soon but served as a switch to open the mic at the door. "Can I come in? I have an urgent matter to discuss with you."

He was tempted to use an override code he wasn't technically supposed to know and force his way in. This was a matter of life and death, and whatever Abby was in the middle of could certainly wait.

"I said just a minute, and I meant it. I already know why you're here."

"If you know that, then you also know that timing could be critical."

"That's why I'd prefer if you'd stop yakking at my door and let me finish up. Let yourself in if you must. It's not locked."

Charlie7 scowled but activated the door release. This wasn't like Abby, who was as jealous of her privacy as any human he'd known since Olivia. 'Quiet was a writer's best friend,' she always said.

"Is something the matter?" Charlie7 asked as he stepped into the quaint foyer decorated in the style of a Victorian sitting room. Dark, polished wood and ornate embroidery contrasted with modern touches such as a video screen and a cybernetics tuning kit left open beneath the shade of a faux-gas lamp.

Abby bustled through the foyer, depositing a suitcase at Charlie7's feet on her way past. "Stow that, if you want to make yourself useful."

"Stow it where?"

"Your skyroamer," Abby replied gruffly. "I presume you're here to take me to Mars."

"Take you?" Charlie7 asked dubiously. "We have a situation on Mars, but we're looking for a negotiator, not a rescue."

Abby called out from down the hall, voice raised but forcing Charlie7 to up the gain on his audio receptors to hear her. "Well, damn good thing you came here since I'm about ninety years past prime rescue mission age. As for negotiating, that business only gets anything done face to face. I haven't been on Mars since they added a second colony dome. Hadn't anticipated ever seeing it again up close and in person. But... well, you know as well as anyone that plans never survive contact with the enemy."

"You... think I'm taking you to Mars?" Charlie7 said. His intention had been to bring her to Philadelphia, where a team of advisers could coach her on the situation and work back channel solutions with the Curiosity officials on site at Arthur Miller Theater.

"Fat lot of good it'll do me talking to them from Earth," Abby said. "Those twitchy brats have had about their fill of transmissions from Earth making promises and telling them what to do. You do this for me: get me carte blanche from the Human Welfare Committee to do what needs doing up there, and I'll leave you in peace to pilot the spaceroamer."

"Are you sure you should be traveling interplanetary—?"

"At my age?" Abby finished for him. "Look here, Charlie7. Those de-evolving apes took my little Kaylee hostage. I'm planning to do whatever it takes to get her out of there safely. She's got a good eighty to a hundred years left to live, and if I have to trade my last few for her to live them, so be it. But I think I'll not shatter like porcelain taking a quick hop over to get there."

Charlie7 just shook his head and carried Abby's bags. She was all fire where Eve was calm and deliberate. Even Eve's anger was less intense than a typical conversation with Earth's premier playwright and author. Ned Lund and his pals were going to have a public relations disaster on their hands if they harmed this particular negotiator.

Abby had all Eve's fame, a way of persuading with words that was as subtle as a tropical breeze, and none of her mother's political baggage. If it weren't for that iron will of Eve's to impose her judgment on others and break their resolve, Abby might have been his first choice to handle negotiations.

As he slung her bags into the back of his skyroamer, now with a short trip home for a spacefaring model as their destination, he wondered at the possibility that the trip would prove too much. If Abby didn't survive the trip to Mars, Charlie7 decided he'd conduct the negotiations personally.

CHAPTER TWENTY-NINE

The inside of Arthur Miller Theater had become a prison straight out of an archival movie. The doors had all been welded shut except for a single back entrance, which the Chain Breakers kept heavily guarded. Kaylee and the other hostages had been herded into the audience seating and told to stay put.

Each of the twelve hostages wore a bomb collar around their neck and a freshly woven, form-fitting, plain white jumpsuit without pockets, courtesy of the cloth-o-matic kept backstage for making costumes. They were barefoot, stripped of jewelry and tech, and wiped with an EMP for good measure.

It hadn't been until the vision in her left eye went completely blurry that Kaylee even remembered the implanted lens in it. It helped her examine tiny details without needing a microscope and had become so second-nature over the course of her adult life that it hadn't occurred to her to worry as Gregor, from turbine control, steadied her in front of the EMP.

Now, blinded in one eye, she sat sullenly in the third row on a plush velvet seat, feet chilled against the concrete floor. Alan sat two seats over, slouched in his seat with his head lolled back and his eyes shut. His hand dangled across the middle seat, an invitation waiting for Kaylee to accept.

Up on stage, Ned and a couple of his buddies conversed too softly for the hostages to hear.

A row behind her, Martha Jameson whispered to Kevin Chang. "You think they'd do it? You think they'd really kill us?"

Kevin hushed her but not fast enough.

"Hey!" Ned shouted, storming over to the edge of the stage. "No talking. You're a bargaining chip, so shut up and act like one."

Kaylee held her breath, gaze locked on the remote in Ned's robot-like grip. Even a slip could kill them all.

There were whimpers behind her. The offenders didn't speak a word of apology or contrition. They just shut up as told.

When Ned turned his attention back to his co-conspirators, she let out a breath.

Beside her, Alan snored softly. She shot him a look of reproach. He didn't even have the decency to be properly terrified with her.

However, in that look, she also noticed the bare line of paler skin where his wedding band had been. She rubbed at the naked spot where her own had been, then at her sore jaw when they'd slugged her for refusing to hand it over. There'd been no need to confiscate them. Kaylee wasn't some secret agent with a transmitter in her ring—or a dark energy blaster or anything else dangerous. Taking their possessions had been an intimidation tactic.

Kaylee wanted to refuse to let it work on her, but it had anyway.

There was a clatter from backstage. Kaylee's hopes rose along with a shot of fear. Was it a raid? Was someone finally coming to rescue them? The Chain Breakers were obviously in contact with the outside but hadn't been forthcoming with details of the situation beyond the theater walls.

"Chow time," Ned announced.

Kaylee's stomach growled. Alan stirred and straightened in his seat. The theater kept a few snacks on hand. Kaylee could have gone for one of the granola bars just then.

Instead, school children filed into the audience, coming down the steps at the sides of the stage. Each bore a tray with a freshly cooked meal. The smells of the meats were tantalizing. None of the young waitstaff could have been over the age of ten.

"Get moving," Ned ordered, spurring the youthful workforce to quicken their pace. "No talking. Keep it moving. Just drop off a tray and get outta here."

Kaylee smiled a silent thanks for hers, which turned out to contain a shaved steak sandwich with cheese, mushrooms, and onions. It was already cut in half, and there was a plastic cup of fruit juice set into a holder at the side of the tray. No utensils. No food that required them. Someone on the outside was thinking, at least.

But as she chewed the first bite, Kaylee realized what this meant. The Chain Breakers weren't planning on letting them go anytime soon. When the young tray-bearers came back minutes later, they were carrying plain white blankets for each hostage, still warm from the cloth-o-matic.

Alan was stuffing his face with his sandwich when Kaylee caught his eye. He reached across the seat between them. Kaylee squeezed his hand.

There was no telling what Ned had in mind, but they were bargaining chips. That much he'd made clear. What sort of bargain he was looking for, Kaylee had only grim guesses, none of them appealing. Worse, she wondered what the Chain Breakers would do to her, Alan, and the rest of the hostages if Ned didn't get what he was looking for.

CHAPTER THIRTY

Hours had passed uncounted. The Chain Breakers had left no computers of any sort for the hostages. The theater had no windows and no clocks. The roughest estimate Kaylee could cobble together was based on how often she needed one of her captors to escort her to the washroom.

She hadn't worked it out to an exact science, but Ned seemed to have ordered his men to allow them one visit apiece every six hours whether they used it or not. But it was only guesswork based on estimates piled upon assumptions founded on yet more estimates.

At least they had relented and allowed the captives to mill around. So long as they kept to the front center section of seating, Kaylee and the others were free to roam.

Down the rows, bare feet slapped on concrete. Kaylee's, Martha's, Fatima's, Casey's... they all made the same public-shower sound pacing the aisles.

Kaylee kept her hands off her collar. Every time they let her use the washroom, they hurried her in and out. But every time, she saw the device reflected in the mirror. The scientist in her demanded she study it, understand it, take control of it. However, with one good eye and scant seconds to wash up after using the toilet, she couldn't begin to unravel the mysteries of the homemade device threatening her life.

"It would be just like me to figure this out and *still* blow my damn head off," Kaylee muttered.

Alan shushed her. She'd walked too close, and he'd overheard.

"Don't you even start," she snapped in a harsh whisper. "We wouldn't be in this mess if not for your amateur heroics."

Glaring plasma torches up from his seat, he spat back, "I just wanted to help Mars! You're the one who wanted to come live here in the first place."

"You two," Ned yelled from the stage. "Shut up!"

"Hey," Kaylee shot back, no longer lowering her voice now that they'd been caught. "It wasn't my idea to play Donnie Brasco like you were a theater student at rehearsal."

"Lower your voice," Alan warned.

Kaylee was having none of it. "Don't hide behind these stupid bombs around our necks. If they wanted to blow us to kibble, they'd have done it by now."

"I said knock it off," Ned ordered. Two of his goons were coming.

Alan scooted down in his seat and put his hands up. His eyes pleaded for Kaylee to quiet down.

"This is *not* the last word on this subject," Kaylee warned as two men lifted her and dragged her down the row. "Put me down. Calvin, you are so fired when this is over."

"Aw, just blow this *one* collar," Calvin whined to Ned up on stage.

"Oh, just knock a few teeth out," Ned suggested as an alternative.

Dulled to the persistent threat of an exploding collar that had yet to go off, Kaylee felt a renewed pang of terror. She'd still be useful as a hostage so long as she was breathing, and there was a long way to go between healthy and dead.

It was a spectrum she didn't relish exploring.

Kicking out with her bare feet, she tried to gain leverage to free herself from the thick-armed captors who held her aloft. Before any of her efforts bore fruit, a fist full of knuckles caught her in the nose and mouth.

Kaylee blacked out.

CHAPTER THIRTY-ONE

The English countryside shone brilliant green late May. Grassy hillsides and leafy forests gave way to the lovingly curated modernity of Oxford School. Red brick facades concealed the most advanced educational facility in the solar system. Two thousand years past, Oxford had educated the academic and political elites of its day. Now, pre-pubescent children with intellects far beyond those ancient scholars filled those dormitories. The parents of two Oxford students were speeding toward the school on an errand neither of them relished.

Lucy Chase fidgeted in the passenger seat of the skyro as Dr. Toby piloted them in for a landing. "What should we tell them?" she asked.

Dr. Toby shrugged, hands steady on the controls with robotic precision at odds with the all-too-human appearance of his chassis. "The truth? Would that be out of line? They're ten and eight. What's the cutoff for telling an unemancipated kid the unvarnished truth?"

"But what good's worrying going to do them?" Lucy asked. "I mean, what if we came up with a plausible white lie? Wouldn't that be kinder?"

"Like what? It's not like they don't have Solarwide access. Unless the teachers blocked coverage, they're bound to have heard something by now."

"You can't imagine..."

"What? That Nora109 would let on that evil isn't consigned to the history books? That humans are a danger to one another?"

"That their parents might be killed by a madman," Lucy said.

"There's no educational value to that. Quite the contrary. They've got their whole futures ahead of them, even if it comes to the worst. What's the use of taking their concentration from their studies?"

"Do you want me to turn this skyro around and head home? I can head home if that's what you'd rather." The vessel banked to the west, the force of the turn pushing Lucy down into the cushion of her seat.

"I didn't say that!" Lucy replied. "What if they haven't told them anything yet?"

"We could call and ask," Dr. Toby suggested for at least the tenth time.

"NO!" Lucy exclaimed. "That would be the worst way for the poor dears to find out that their parents are hostages. And we can't check with the school to know; if it wasn't a faculty decision, they could have found out from practically anyone."

"You're over-thinking this," Dr. Toby said calmly. It was easy for him to say. He had literal coolant for blood. He didn't have to deal with fear for the fragile little psyches of their grandchildren. *He* could look at everything rationally if he chose. "Let's just show up and hug them."

Lucy snorted her opinion of that plan. Child psychology was hardly invented back in the Human Era. The barbarism of his own upbringing prior to his brain scan was the stuff of nightmares. That he'd turned into a decent, productive member of society was a testament to the human spirit and ability to overcome adversity.

By God, they'd forced him to play piano against his will.

There was no time for regressive thinking. Not now. Lucy had raised Alan to be a sound, rational young man, and he'd raised his own children the same way. Kaylee's free-spirited streak notwithstanding, Athena and Stephen were on solid footing to deal with whatever tragedy might befall their parents.

The skyro parked in the visitors' lot at Oxford amid a sea of similar models. Some curmudgeonly mixed robots might not upgrade their skyro for twenty years or more at a time, but any parent with children at Oxford wouldn't be caught in anything older than a few years.

Lucy and Dr. Toby made their way to the dormitory main entrance and checked in at the visitors' kiosk. A quick ID scan allowed them access to the student level where Athena and Stephen both roomed in opposite wings.

But they didn't have to split up or choose which child to visit first. They were right in the common lounge between the girls' and boys' wings. They looked bigger every time Lucy saw them, impossibly shaping into closer and closer doppelgangers of their own parents.

At the sight of them, both youngsters came running. "Grammy Lucy, Grampy Toby!" they shouted.

Left in the childrens' wake, another pair of grandparents accepted their displacement with casual aplomb. Wendy Fourteen raised a hand. "You should have called. We could have come together."

As the two sides of the family came together, Lucas Truman shook Dr. Toby's hand. "Shouldn't take bad news for us to get together."

Lucy ignored Wendy and gathered Athena and Stephen in her arms. "You two been good for your other grammy and grampy?"

"Yeah," Stephen assured her.

"I'm always good," Athena bragged, casting Stephen a look implying that he clearly was not.

"How are they taking it?" Dr. Toby asked quietly, but if Lucy could overhear, so could the children.

Wendy heaved a sigh. "We've done our best to prepare them, but there's never anything that can stop it hurting."

"She's a trooper, though," Lucas said, his wan smile making a vain attempt at reassurance.

Lucy scowled and didn't try to hide it. "Alan's every bit as tough. Beneath that sensitive exterior, he's got a core of iron."

"Just like the Earth?" Stephen asked, obviously having studied geology recently enough to recall the Earth's ferromagnetic interior.

"I don't think we're talking about the same thing," Wendy said, raising one eyebrow. "We were picking them up to go visit their great-great-grandmother in the hospital. She... asked for them." By Wendy's hesitation, Lucy knew that boded ill for the old chairwoman's prospects.

Dr. Toby cleared his throat. "We've come about the... other situation."

Lucas chuckled. "Don't worry about that business on Mars. Nasty stuff, but it'll blow over. Heck, I'll build them a damn reactor if that's what it takes."

"Violence is destructive and counterproductive," Athena recited, straight out of the Oxford Code of Conduct.

"They... know?" Lucy asked warily.

"It's OK," Stephen reassured her. "They sent Great Grammy up to Mars. When she gets there, she'll fix it all."

This was the first Lucy was hearing of an envoy being sent. "That's not on the news feeds. Who told you this?"

"Mom sent me a just-in-case list, things to take care of if she's... gone a while," Wendy said. "But I'm sure she'll handle everything just fine."

"Woman her age ought to get waited on hand and foot," Lucy said, not without the smallest bit of self-interest. She'd greatly appreciate some pampering some forty years hence. "You'd think an interplanetary trip would wear her to the bone. What's to say those hooligans aren't in the mood for clever chatter?"

"Well," Wendy said with a forced-friendly smile. "Well, I imagine that's why she had Charlie7 bring her. Kaylee and Alan are walking out of that Martian theater one way or another. Those so-called Neddites... Mom's their best chance."

Lucas herded the kids toward the exit. "C'mon. We told Great-Great-Grammy Eve we'd be there by noon, Philadelphia time. Don't want to keep her waiting."

The two children picked up the pace of their departure instantly. "Why can't she be in the hospital in Paris?" Stephen asked.

As the other half of the family disappeared beyond audible range, the last comment Lucy heard was Wendy's flippant reply. "There are still a couple things Great-Great-Grammy Eve can't order around. And believe me, she tries."

CHAPTER THIRTY-TWO

The sonorous hum of the spacero's engine was the only sound during the interplanetary transit. Abby knew that they'd have been accelerating harder if Charlie7 had been alone in the cockpit. For the latter half of the trip, they'd have to turn the vehicle around for the decelerating force to press her frail human body against the seat cushion rather than strain her neck and dig the safety restraints into her chest.

"You awake over there?" Charlie7 asked casually.

"My eyes are open, aren't they?" Abby replied. "Hasn't been *that* long since you were human, has it?"

"Well, Eve has the same implants, and she sometimes—"

"I'm not Mom," Abby replied. "These are just eyes. Same hardware, maybe, but I don't keep them hooked into every bodily system and the Solarwide to boot."

"I always assumed..."

"Because I never talk about it," Abby replied. "Last thing Mom needs is for the anti-roboticists to add a 'but her daughter has the same cyber eyes and doesn't use them as a terminal.' I let people gossip. Never hurts an artiste to have an air of mystery, no matter how slight."

"Anyway, since you *are* awake, I was going to suggest you eat something."

"Rather you keep accelerating," Abby replied. "I'll eat later."

"It's a long trip. You'll need at least five meals."

Abby shut her eyes. It lessened the desire to fix a glare on the busybody robot, which would have required more neck strength than she possessed as the spacero shot through the void. As it was, at best she might strain a muscle trying.

"Or nap," Charlie7 said. "Save your strength. You're going to need it."

"Either you think I'm sleeping, and you should cut power to your voice modulator, or I'm just resting my eyes, and you can stop patronizing me. I'm old, not incompetent."

"Fine. You're awake. Maybe it's a good time to start planning a strategy."

"Showing up and negotiating *is* the strategy."

"Well, broadly, I suppose. I was thinking of perhaps taking it one step deeper and coming up with obstacles and countermeasures."

Abby sighed. Despite Charlie7 upping the oxygen mix in the cockpit, the force pressing her against the seat made it work to breathe. "My plan is to ask them what they're after—really after, not the ridiculous list they sent to goad us—and work to see how little of it I can give them to release everyone unharmed. If they give me any guff, I intend to be charming as hell until they can't stand it any longer."

"That... might work."

Abby wasn't some young kitten to have a string dangled in front of her. "If you want to say something, say it. I am, as you might imagine, a captive audience."

"Do you plan on meeting them face to face?"

"If possible. I find the stage more engaging than any recorded performance. More like stand-up comedy than a sitcom."

"I never cared for your stand-up, if we're being honest," Charlie7 said.

"We all need to learn our strengths and weaknesses," Abby countered. "Not all of us programmed ourselves to be perfect."

"I'm just saying that we ought to consider the possibility that things don't go smoothly. If you're conducting in-person negotiations, we might need to formulate a rescue plan before they get one of those collars onto you and add you to their menagerie."

"They've got my granddaughter. I'll risk whatever it takes to secure her safety. No putting Kaylee and the others in danger. I utterly forbid you to try anything involving force."

"I'm sure I can come up with a plan that involves minimal risk. If I convince the Martian colonial authorities to give me use of five or six of their construction drones—"

"Forbid."

"But what if—"

"Look here, Rasputin," Abby said darkly. "These are humans. Frail, ephemeral, infinitely valuable. They don't get reloaded into a spare chassis if someone kills them. They didn't back up their consciousness to a secret archive somewhere just before leaving Earth. Go ahead and deny it."

Charlie7 remained silent but eased off the throttle a hair for her benefit.

"You see, I've got to weigh however many years I've got left against the innumerably more years those poor hostages might experience. And it doesn't help that I might save my granddaughter only to lose my mother while I'm off on another planet. But I had to choose between possibly seeing my mother one last time and maybe being the difference in my grandbaby getting to keep on living."

"I'm just trying to be objective."

"Well, stop it," Abby concluded. She opened her eyes, staring ahead into the star-flecked darkness. Mars was one of those tiny glows up ahead, though it was too soon to pick out which. "This is the time to feel out the humanity in another person, dig deep into the hurt that's causing them to lash out, and patch up the differences. Corollary to getting all the hostages out alive is that I've got to find a way for all the hostage takers to come away satisfied."

"You should still eat something."

"Changing the subject is an admission of defeat."

Abby closed her eyes again and drifted off for a nap, knowing that Charlie7 wouldn't interfere with her plans.

CHAPTER THIRTY-THREE

Kaylee was losing track of days. Her best guess as to how long the siege had lasted was based around an assumption that they were getting three meals a day delivered by children from the outside. But there was no confirmation of that assumption, and the hostage takers hadn't enforced any type of schedule. The theater lights remained on around the clock, and the captors themselves napped in rotating shifts.

"They could have left us a checkerboard, a deck of cards, anything," Fatima Sharif muttered as she paced her aisle. Territories had formed over the course of the hostages' stay, with Kaylee and Alan sharing adjacent rows of seating.

"Quiet down there," Calvin shouted from the stage.

Ned was too busy on his portable to bother with them. Kaylee strained her ears but couldn't make out the faintest hint of even one side of the conversation.

What was taking so long?

Had Ned demanded that Earth send people over to finish the terraforming before he'd let them all go?

Five rows back from Kaylee, Casey Laramie screamed. It wasn't a shriek of terror or a bellow of rage. By Kaylee's guess at the dome maintenance engineer's demeanor over the past few hours, she figured it was pent-up frustration. The scream ended, only to be followed by an intake of air and a repetition.

"Knock it off," Calvin ordered. When the scream became almost a mantra, Calvin came down to the seating area slapping a heavy wrench against the palm of his hand. "All right. Hard way it is."

The other hostages ducked for cover, hunkering down between the rows or cowering in their seats. But Kaylee couldn't just sit there. The isolation was taking its toll on their captors as well. Calvin had the bloodshot eyes of a man not getting enough sleep, and the look in them promised murder.

Kaylee scrambled over seat backs, racing to get to Casey before Calvin and his wrench arrived. She tripped. She banged her knees and ankles. She kept moving.

Despite lips that were still swollen from her beating days ago, she called out to the Chain Breaker. "Don't hurt him! I'll get him to stop."

Calvin was in no hurry. There was nowhere for anyone to run. His weary nonchalance in meting out corporal punishment allowed Kaylee to win the race. She pulled Casey up by the shoulders and looked him in the eye. There was madness there, the look of a trapped animal in a panic to escape a room with no exit.

"Casey," Kaylee whispered. "Calm down."

He screamed in her face.

Kaylee pulled him against her, muffling his screams against her chest. She turned the two of them so it was she who faced down the stalking Chain Breaker. If Calvin wanted to beat Casey into silence, he was going to have to tear him away from Kaylee to do it.

She locked gazes with the man. Calvin had been a coworker, though nothing like a friend. She'd held a senior position on the Mars Terraforming Initiative. Maybe some innate respect for that hierarchy slowed his pace as Calvin drew near.

Kaylee knew from her occasional visits to the washroom how she looked. Two blackened eyes. Adhesive bandage splayed across a splinted nose. Bruises and welts sprayed slapdash with temporary skin. Her lips puffed like she'd been stung by a wasp.

But the eyes.

During those brief visits, she'd practiced in the mirror. She had the eyes for it. Kaylee had the identical genome, after all. If Eve could cow a six-hundred-year-old robot with a look, Kaylee ought to be able to get a thirty-something ventilation mechanic to back down.

Dull resentment glowered back at Kaylee from those bloodshot eyes. Calvin slowed his approach until he stopped at the end of the aisle, not setting foot between the seats. "Get out of the way."

"He's calmed down," Kaylee replied, not so much as blinking. "Go pretend to care about humans somewhere else."

She hoped that Casey blocked Calvin's view of her heaving chest. Let him focus on her eyes, where all Kaylee's anger and willpower was focused. She dreaded him coming down the aisle and bludgeoning her with that wrench, but she couldn't allow him to see that anxiety in her. Animals could smell fear, but she had to hope Calvin hadn't devolved that far.

He was human, same as her—the animal without instinct. The sole biological creature with a fully developed cognitive mind.

Calvin inclined his head. "Fine. You just keep him quiet, or it's the both of you next time."

CHAPTER THIRTY-FOUR

Social drinking establishments had come and gone in Paris since the population explosion of the Second Human Era. The successful ones seemed always to follow the styling of an old English or Irish pub despite the Parisian setting. They were places that humans from different social circles could gather to discuss the latest items from the news feeds over a drink to loosen inhibitions. Today, those casual debates centered on the standoff on Mars.

A veterinarian turned to the children's game programmer beside her. "Nuts what's happening in Curiosity." A silent video screen above the bar showed images on transmit-only delay from the colony standoff. Colonial officials camped out in a tent headquarters beyond the safety cordon while the colonists went about daily life behind them.

The programmer gasped after a long swig of his stout. "Can't keep the breeders from fouling the gene pool. Did you know every single one of those Neddites was human-birthed?"

"No kidding?" the veterinarian replied. She shook her head. "Human Welfare ought to just approve a little snippity-snip at puberty. Save the babies for the geneticists who know what they're doing."

The programmer grunted. "Wouldn't catch me practicing unregulated genetics. My two came pressed and cleaned from the labs. Little angels, the both of them."

Across fifty-five million kilometers of empty space, the same topic held the attention of two workers at a hydroponics farm on the outskirts of the Discovery colony. They crouched on opposite sides of a row of tomato basins that ran the fifty-meter length of the enclosure.

"You hoping they get what they're asking for?" the nutrient engineer asked her coworker.

The botanist scowled at the leaf of a tomato plant through his data monocle. "Can't say that I condone their actions. Be nice to take a stroll outside, though. Earthlings take it for granted, but I want to own an open-cockpit skyro and take the wife out on weekend flights for the sheer joy of it."

"You'd have to learn to pilot a skyro."

"You saying I couldn't?"

"I've seen you drive a rover."

They shared a chuckle at the botanist's expense and forgot about the hostages for the rest of the shift.

In the bowels of the great factory at Kanto, Jason90 and Kabir3 held a debate of their own by the new assembly line for Version 92 chassis.

"Can't wait to hop into one of these," Kabir3 said admiringly, watching the blank, customizable base units file past.

Most of the chassis would be fitted for a new line of household drones, servants in the style of old feudal estates, enough for every human to have his own attending butler or maid. The best off the line would be set aside for the Upload Committee to assign new robots in need of upgrade. Kabir3 wasn't in line for a new chassis for decades yet, but Jason90 didn't begrudge him the dream.

"I may hold out for the next functional model," Jason90 replied.

Kabir3 shook his head. "You've been mechanical too long. Don't you want the upgraded sensory input?"

"Frankly, I don't have time to waste on a chassis that's less capable than my current 68.9. I want a Truman-Effect reactor, but the reduced speed and power output on the human-real models will probably never appeal to me. There's always going to be more function if you cut out the form requirements."

"You worried about Martian rebels?" Kabir3 teased. "Afraid you might get punked like Brent104?"

"Brent104's old enough to know his limits better than that," Jason90 said coldly. "Makes the rest of us look bad panicking and hurting the biologicals."

"A disease," Kabir3 said. "Brent104 ought to have put a few down like rabid vermin. The population's small enough that we can still stamp out failed sub-populations before they breed beyond containment."

"You talking families or entire colonies?" Jason90 asked dryly. He set down a microcrystallurgy scanner to wait for his underling's response.

"There are Social algorithms to tell who the real troublemakers are. I bet there are a dozen robots who could sift the Solarwide and put names to all the anonymous IDs floating around."

"And then what? Incinerators, like the old human cloners? That was before your time, but I don't think that's an answer."

Kabir3 took the scanner and held it up. "Imagine if we had one of these that could look inside a human brain and pick out the bad ones."

"Excellent," Jason90 replied. "Genocide with surgical precision. Knock it off with that bullshit, and get back to work."

Kabir3 giggled, forcing Jason90 to wonder whether the younger robot was serious or just needling him. Jason90 snatched back the scanner with a scowl and headed down the line to check power usage on the conveyor line.

The Cutting Edge Science Committee was no longer in session. The members had been dismissed, but many lingered in the halls outside the meeting chamber.

"What would be the impact if we did just give Mars the next three full-scale Truman-Effect reactors?" John77 asked.

Keith Newman shook his head. "Bad precedent. Even if it had *no* effect on Kanto's new project—and I fully support no-recharge robot chassis—we can't go letting antisocial hotheads dictate our priorities."

"We have oversight committees for that," Jena Einstein deadpanned to a chorus of muted chuckles.

"I heard the crew of that transorbital parked at Curiosity has gone silent," Marvin220 said. "I bet they're coordinating with Charlie7 on some sort of hostage rescue. This whole discussion is moot if the situation gets resolved without giving in to any demands."

A different pair of robots on far-off Mars was the subject of a quiet conversation between their human counterparts. The four of them were performing surveying work for the proposed Viking-1 colony, the first to be built for open-air habitation. While the robots on the surveying team wore normal outerwear, Jesse and Gale wore full environmental suits to protect against the cold and the thin, oxygen-poor atmosphere.

Their attire also came with radios that could be tuned to a private channel just for the two of them.

"You think they ever wonder about us?" Gale asked. "You know, they could be having whole side conversations even while talking right to our faces."

"I try not to. Rather just get this sewage line roughed out and measured and call it a day."

"What would we even do if they just came over and yanked the power supply out of our breathers?" Gale pressed. "I mean, we wouldn't see it coming. If we did, I doubt we could stop them."

"I can talk to Bruce about putting you back on a dome-side assignment," Jesse suggested. "I don't mind being out here with them."

"Braver man than I am..."

"Look, just because I don't want them on Mars doesn't mean they're murderers. For now, we've got a job to do, so shut up and quit bothering me."

While all this was going on, a small family reunion was taking place in Philadelphia. Eve lay in bed, eyes kept open by a tiny mechanical hinge so she could see. Utterly exhausted, it had taken all her considerable influence to convince the nursing staff to give her a neurostimulant for the visit.

The hiss of the breathing apparatus doing her lungs' work for her filled every silence.

"*You both look beautiful,*" a box perched on Eve's lap said on her behalf, addressing Athena and Stephen, who sat at the foot of the bed unsure of what to do with themselves. They'd been forbidden to hug their great-great-grandmother, and holding her hand would have prevented the limited communication she was still capable of.

Behind the children, their grandparents—Eve's granddaughter and grandson-in-law—stood with brave smiled riveted to their faces.

"You're getting them out of calculus class," Wendy informed her.

"Are you worried about Mom and Dad?" Stephen asked.

Eve had to admit, she felt uneasy allowing Abby to go in her place. Five years younger and no force in the solar system would have stopped her from getting on a spaceroamer and flying straight over to Mars.

All it would have taken was a quick message to Charlie7. It could have been brief, terse to the point of presumptuous, and utterly violating the sanctity of committee-based decision-making. Charlie7 would have caught hell for obeying, but he'd have done it. "Take care of it." That's all Eve would have needed.

"Yes," Eve said via the speaker box. "But my Abby has a good heart. She'll make them see reason."

Eve wished that what might prove her final visit with these young, precious children wouldn't be colored by lies.

CHAPTER THIRTY-FIVE

The spacero bearing Abby and Charlie7 passed through the airlock and into a reserved parking area within the Curiosity dome. There was already a rover waiting for them when they touched down, sent ahead by the colonial authorities to expedite Abby's arrival.

"Welcome to Curiosity, Madame negotiator," a man in a drab gray jumpsuit greeted her, offering a hand stepping down from the cockpit.

Even the foreign Martian gravity felt absolutely delightful after the disconcerting artificial sort imposed by the skyro's thrusters. No sooner had they accelerated to their maximum speed but the damned robot had spun them backward, powered up to the max thrust Abby could stand once again, and slowed them down for arrival.

She knew how interplanetary transit worked, but that didn't make the rough voyage any easier on the innards.

"Washroom," Abby commanded.

The attendant held out a hand toward the skyro. "But..."

"I know it comes with one. I used the damned thing eleven times and held my bladder to planetfall before the twelfth. Quit arguing with me about how many times a 127-year-old woman ought to let a robot hear her tinkle and show me to a washroom."

"I'd do as she asked," Charlie7 advised, circling around from the other side of the craft with its engines still winding down. "She's been cranky the past five million kilometers or so."

There was a maintenance shed for the landing yard. It had all the facilities Abby needed. It was a nice change from the past days, with all the gravitational forces heading toward their proper axes. The normalcy was the real pleasure she took. Tiny biological oddities like that bound mankind in common experience.

Minutes later, she and Charlie7 were in the back of the attendant's rover.

"I didn't catch your name," Abby said over the rumble of the tires on the colony roads.

"Ahmed, ma'am," the driver said. "An honor to meet you."

Ahmed, she thought to herself. She wracked her brain for a connection to that name. "Class of 3201?" she ventured.

"3202," Ahmed replied. "Didn't expect you'd remember me."

"You were shorter," Abby said. "Something in your smile stayed since your emancipation. You end up going into astronomy?"

"Gave it up after a few years in orbit. Found out I like gravity more than mapping distant galaxies."

Never forget the people in between. Many of Abby's plays held onto that theme, that between the criminals and the leaders of nations lay the meat and sinew of mankind.

When they arrived at Arthur Miller Theater, Abby allowed Ahmed to help her out of the rover. Instantly, the colonial authorities swarmed to her.

"Ms. Abbigail," Dana Platt said as she took the liberty of a rather one-sided handshake. "Once the Chain Breakers got word you were on the way, they stopped communicating except for sending in humanitarian supplies."

"Why would you do a thing like that?" Charlie7 asked. "Should have just starved them out. This would have been over days ago."

"None of that," Abby scolded. "Madame mayor, I'd like to head inside and deal with Ned Lund directly."

Dana was aghast. "We'll get you a channel to negotiate with them. They've been very specific that no one is to enter or leave except pre-emancipated children and only then to bring meals."

"Anyone monitoring the waste lines for messages?" Charlie7 asked. "Scrawled notes, data chips, anything that might have been smuggled out to give additional intel on the hostage takers."

Abby turned to the robot. "Would you mind letting me handle this?" She beckoned to Dana. "Give me the portable that can talk to Ned Lund. The first thing I'll be negotiating is a way inside."

No one bothered explaining the setup of the portable or the protocols for dealing with hostage takers. No one dared. There were plays yet to be written and many a bumbling, playwright-patronizing buffoon to be written in and immortalized in infamy.

"Hello, I'd like to speak with Edward Lund," she said formally.

"This is Ned," came the gruff reply. Unlike Ahmed at the landing yard, this voice didn't conjure memories of a child from Oxford. Ned Lund was Martian to the bone, never having set foot on Earth as best Abby could discover. *"Who's this?"*

Abby raised an eyebrow despite being on voice-only communication. She supposed that she *did* sound like her genetic twins, although *she* could tell an Eve from a Wendy from a Kaylee just fine. Her aunts had all been so distinctive in her mind that it was hard to imagine anyone actually confusing them in conversation. It wasn't as if *Eve's* voice was unfamiliar to anyone.

Whether Ned was playing at being dense or came by it naturally, Abby played along. "This is Abbigail Fourteen, authorized negotiator on behalf of... well, pretty much anyone you'd care to deal with."

"You have my list of demands?" Ned asked.

"Yes," Abby replied. "Have you got mine?"

There was a momentary pause. *"Your demands? I don't think you get how this works."*

"Of course, I do," Abby said in a huff. "You want things. I want things. We haggle until neither of us thinks they can do any better, and a deal gets done."

"If you've got the list, then I suggest you start checking things off."

"My demands are these," Abby pressed. She strolled away from a gaggle of eavesdropping busybodies who could damn well wait for a transcript once she was done. "I want a doctor to examine the hostages."

"Denied."

"I want you to release anyone in need of medical attention that cannot be satisfactorily provided within the confines of a theater," Abby continued.

"Denied. And you're getting on my nerves."

"Lastly, I want to conduct future negotiations face-to-face. I think we'd both benefit from a better understanding of whom we are dealing with. You're a populist, Mr. Lund. A man of the people must know that hurting anyone undermines your very purpose for being."

"OK. No more Mr. Nice Guy. I'd been saving this for Eve Fourteen, but since it sounds like she's too much a coward to come to Mars herself, I'll flush it down your garbage chute. You know that missing transorbital crew?"

Abby's mouth went dry. "I was aware there was a vessel docked at Curiosity."

"I've got them. Five total. Completely helpless—just the heads hooked up to a backup power supply. You've got one hour to start showing progress, or I start wiping brains... nice, sterile, non-human brains."

CHAPTER THIRTY-SIX

Charlie7 watched stoically as the humans fell to pieces around him. Abby stared blankly at the screen after the video ended. They'd all seen the five decapitated robotic heads, eyes all aglow, dangling wires that ran outside the camera's field of view. The Martian officials babbled orders into their portables and argued over courses of action.

The clock had kept running on the fate of the robots as inquiries to Earth, visual comparisons to known chassis imperfections, and sending a team to search the transorbital ate away seconds and minutes.

"I'd had hoped he was all bluster," Abby said when the shock wore off enough for her to speak. "How can you champion human independence and sacrifice human lives to get it? But this...? This I can see coming all too clearly."

"Seventeen minutes left," Charlie7 said. "We can rig up an incapacitating audio pulse, maybe anesthetize via the ventilation system. We can go in with a stealth team and use tranquilizer darts. That's three scenarios where no one gets more than a minor injury. Pick one."

Dana shook her head. "I can't have that on my conscience. If anything goes wrong, that's twenty human lives and five robotic existences that—"

"Lives," Charlie7 interrupted testily. "The robots are alive too."

"Of course, but—"

"No buts," Charlie7 said. "This is Abby's call to make."

Abby shook her head. "We need more time. I need to get inside there. Maybe if we meet *one* of his demands, he'll at least spare the robots."

"Optimistic," Dana said. "What if it doesn't?"

"He's asking for the keys to the planet," Abby snapped. "We can't exactly do that, and he knows it. It's a bargaining position. We need a show of good faith. What's on that list?"

Charlie7 remembered a time when Abby's mind was like a data crystal. However, he understood the grinding effect that age had on the mind even if it was only by decades of observation. Dutifully, he read them off. "The return of the Truman-Effect reactor originally designated for Curiosity Terraforming Site-2, an extensive list of processed ores, the repatriation of all Martian-born children attending Oxford, five seats on the Human Welfare Committee to be voted on and filled by Martian natives, and Martian control of two asteroid mining vessels."

Abby pursed her lips. Charlie7 tried to imagine the machinations going on inside that head. Eve was the pragmatist, the strategist; she understood the human soul like an abacus. Abby was a dreamer, a writer, a teller of stories. While Charlie7 could envision the options Eve might concoct, he had to admit a blind spot for Abby's way of thinking.

"Let's give him the mining vessels," Abby said firmly.

Charlie7 rebooted his audio receptors. "Try that again? I think I misheard."

"There are plenty of them," Abby said. "Plus, it doesn't do lasting damage. We can always claim them back. Deals made under duress are never enforceable."

"But it could be months before another comes back," Dana pointed out.

Charlie7 seriously considered evicting the mayor from her own planning tent. "I believe that would be the whole point. We can give him the main remote access codes. The crew will disembark and seek alternate transport back to Earth. Ned Lund can crew the damn things himself."

Abby nodded. "Good. Get me those codes on my portable, and I'll relay them."

The mayor sighed. "Very well. I'll contact—"

"There you go," Charlie7 said.

Abby glanced down at her portable. "Good. Thanks."

Dana scowled up at Charlie7. "And where, might I ask, did you get access to those codes?"

Once in a while, it didn't hurt to remind them all who they were dealing with. "I built them. Designed them from scratch when Kanto wasn't a tenth the size it is now. I came up with the engines that would allow a vessel that size to enter atmosphere. I programmed them to seek particular ores—it was the asteroid belt between Mars and Jupiter in those days—and bring it back to me. So, I baked in codes that'll let me override manual control. So, what? It's not like I'm even handing over the *good* codes. I can still take back remote access to—"

"Do you mind?" Abby broke in, covering the microphone pickup on her portable. "I'm about to call in. Shoo. Outside. I only want one voice in this negotiation on each side."

Charlie7 complied, holding the tent flap for Dana as a gesture of conciliation. But as soon as they were outdoors, Charlie7 cranked up the gain on his audio receptors.

He filtered out nearby chatter from the weary public safety officials keeping the area clear. An inverse wave dispersed the ambient noise. Dana kept up a string of small talk and nervous chatter that Charlie7 delegated to a subroutine for responses.

All that was left was eavesdropping on Abby's call with Ned Lund.

"*Ned here,*" he answered gruffly.

"You win," Abby said.

"*Well... that's... great. Just great. When are my people getting onto the Human Welfare Committee, then?*"

"Let's not be hasty," Abby replied fluidly. She really did have a finely honed sense of timing, no doubt thanks to her improvisational performances. "You've won a battle. War's got to go on a bit longer. Opening salvo nets you two transorbital of your very own. Ship IDs and override codes are yours as soon as I speak with Kaylee to know she's all right."

"*Nice try. Dummy codes for a conversation with your granddaughter? Not a chance. I need real results. You've got eight minutes left.*"

"Fine. Codes first," Abby said. "But when they check out, I want to talk to Kaylee. You don't get a single thing more out of us until we have word from her that she and the hostages are OK."

"*Couldn't have given me access to the one already docked here?*"

"Your deadline forced us to cut corners," Abby admitted. "Those were the first two codes we could scrounge up."

Charlie7 hid his smirk. That wasn't technically true. He could have given over any transorbital in the fleet. Nothing got transported across the solar system without his implicit consent. Any vessel made in Kanto came with encoding buried so deep that no one could get it out—not without reinventing half of modern technology from the ground up. He'd be damned if he gave that Lund character control of a vessel with more engine power than the entire Martian colonial effort combined. Let him wait months for the ships to return before he gets any use out of them.

"It'll be hours until these codes transmit. Hours before I get confirmation back."

"Well, it was a pretty stupid demand on your part, given your time constraints," Abby said. "But since I don't expect this standoff to end in the next twelve hours, how about you let me talk to my granddaughter on good faith?"

Charlie7 nodded along, feigning agreement with whatever his subroutine was discussing with the Curiosity mayor. Good. Establish an act of faith. That might get Ned Lund to let his guard down.

"All right. Fine. If this turns out to be a stalling tactic, someone's going to regret it."

"Yes, yes, just put Kaylee on," Abby said. "I didn't come all this way to talk to *you*."

An urge welled up in Charlie7. He knew he could send off a signal to those two transorbitals, blocking the override and faking the compliance Ned would demand of them. The vessels might sit out there in the cold, sparse void, their crews never even noticing the tug of war over their ships' loyalties.

He decided to mop up the mess later. Less chance of any deception being sniffed out if there wasn't any to begin with. It wouldn't stop a determinedly paranoid individual, but Ned Lund struck Charlie7 as more disgruntled than disconnected from reality.

"Gram? Is that you?" Kaylee Fourteen asked. There were fine slices of audio interpretive code for telling the difference between all the various Eve clones. Simple inference from context ought to have been enough, but his algorithm was reliable. Abby was savvy enough an impersonator to fool him intentionally, but without conscious effort, he could tell one from the next.

"Kaylee, sweetie, are you all right?" Abby asked. "Have they mistreated you?"

"I'll live," Kaylee replied curtly. Charlie7 had never heard her quite so ragged and raw, but this was her first time as a hostage, he supposed.

"Good girl. Just don't push them too far. Anyone in there badly hurt? In need of a doctor? Is the food getting to you?"

"I'm worst off, and I'll manage. The theater had some first aid supplies. That's been enough. Food's better than the cafeteria at work. Boredom is the

killer. And the uncertainty. I don't even know how long they've kept us in here."

"That's it. I'm getting you out of there. Cognitive dissociation is unhealthy, and you've got a good brain in that skull of yours. I love you, sweetie, but put the thug back on the line."

Charlie7 wondered what she was up to. Kaylee didn't sound like she was suffering even the earliest symptoms of psychological trauma, at least nothing that the initial shock of captivity wouldn't have already triggered.

"I heard that. I'm not deaf, and I'm not stupid. No way I was letting that call be private. I'm not handing over Kaylee Fourteen until—"

"Take me," Abby said quickly.

Charlie7 shut down his small-talk subroutine mid-sentence.

That was it. That was the gambit. He burst into motion, heading straight for the tent. "Don't you dare!" he warned Abby. There were times for heroic gestures. For instance, they were wonderful when carried out by someone you weren't trying to keep alive, preferably an enemy.

"Who's that with you?" Ned asked. *"Don't tell me you dragged Charlie Double-Oh-Seven up here with you. And if he doesn't want you to trade places with Kaylee, then it's a deal. Maybe I just had leverage on the wrong negotiator."*

"Oh, I'll still be negotiating," Abby assured him. "I'm just going to be doing it face-to-face." She shut off the portable before Ned could get the last word.

"What did you just do?" Charlie7 demanded. "Kaylee was a high-value hostage already due to her relationship to Eve. The only one Ned Lund would rather have a hold of in there would be your mother herself."

Abby smiled and headed off in the direction of the theater cordon. "He thinks that now..."

CHAPTER THIRTY-SEVEN

Kaylee fretted more in the minutes following that call from her grandmother than she had the prior several days. Even without overhearing Gram's side of the conversation, Ned's reaction had said it all.

Of all her illustrious relatives—genetic twins or otherwise—possibly only the legendary Plato Fourteen had been more prone to spectacular failures than her grandmother Abbigail. As a creative genius, the ability to have a piece of art bomb spectacularly and keep on going was an invaluable asset.

Kaylee just hoped that she'd fare better with actual bombs involved.

It wasn't that Kaylee was ungrateful. But as she paced the confines of her aisle wringing her hands, she wished that her great-grandmother had come in person. No one was better qualified to handle a tough negotiation than Eve Fourteen.

"All right, Earth girl," Ned said, coming down from the stage. "Let's get moving."

"Moving?" Kaylee asked. "Where?"

"Out," Ned replied. "Free. Pick up the pace before I change my mind."

She looked to her husband. "And Alan?"

"Just go," Alan told her. "I'll be fine."

"Depends how much this one can do from outside," Ned said, hooking a thumb at Kaylee.

Ned marched her out of the audience seating and up the step at the side of the stage, towing her by the upper arm. Kaylee complied readily if not eagerly, pausing before being hauled backstage to share a last glimpse of Alan. He gave her a brave nod.

In the clutches of the Chain Breakers, all by herself, Kaylee wondered whether the promise of freedom was merely a ruse to separate her from the other hostages with minimal fuss. They could do anything to her back here, and there was no one to stop them.

"Hold still," Ned ordered, forcing her into a chair that was little more than a stool with a short backrest.

Kaylee shut her eyes and steadied her breathing, trying to will her imagination into silence. It was just her, Ned, Gregor, and Wil in the room. The calculating, scientific portion of her brain tried to work out how long her ordeal might last if they took turns having their way with her. The lobe responsible for self-preservation told that dispassionate part to shut up and try to remain positive.

She felt hands on her shoulders. "Chin up," Gregor ordered.

A moment later, the collar came free of her neck.

Kaylee opened her eyes. "That's it?"

Ned shoved a bundle into her hands. "That's it. Now get out."

They didn't manhandle her, but Ned and Wil escorted her to the main entrance, where Calvin had been posted as a guard just inside the door. When the door opened, the sting of sunlight glinting through the Curiosity dome stabbed her eyes. She raised a hand to ward away the glare.

A hand squeezed her shoulder. "It'll be all right, dear. Don't worry about me."

Kaylee whirled to see Grammy Abby heading into Arthur Miller Theater in Ned's custody. She reached back, but the door closed, shutting her away.

"Gram, no!" Kaylee shouted, realizing all too late the price of her release.

It was Charlie7's turn to herd Kaylee along by the arm. "Come on. Too many ears by that door," he said in an undertone.

"She can't do that," Kaylee protested quietly, suddenly aware of the eyes following her from just beyond the cordon. There must have been a hundred Martians gathered to view the spectacle of her release.

Dana greeted them as Charlie7 lifted the flimsy yellow plastic strip that marked the no-man's land between Curiosity colony and its tiny breakaway republic of Arthur Miller Theater. She took Kaylee's hands in both of hers. "I'm so glad you're all right. What can you tell us about the situation in there?"

Kaylee did her best to be thorough. She gave them the layout of the hostages and Chain Breakers, the clothing they'd been given, how the meals had been delivered, and their treatment by Ned's goons. If it wasn't already apparent by her face, the latter hadn't been gentle.

"The worst part was the collars," Kaylee said, running a hand along her neck where chafed skin felt the cool breeze of the colony air circulators even inside the tent. "Knowing they could kill us with the touch of a button was terrifying." She didn't want to admit that the very idea of it still was, or that she bore that terror on Alan's behalf even from outside the theater.

"What can you tell us about the devices?" Charlie7 asked. "Anything at all about the control scheme, the type of explosive in them, how the remote works?"

"Ned has a handheld remote," Kaylee said. She described the device but couldn't give much detail beyond a visual description.

"Not much to go on," Dana said. "We can't mount a rescue based on that."

"We *need* to rescue them," Kaylee said. "Ned's not going to cave. He's pathologically averse to giving up. He's a plow ox with a field ahead of him, and he's going to plow it one way or another. I don't think anyone but Eve could talk him out of this insanity. Why *isn't* my great-grandmother here? It's not like her to send someone."

Charlie7 cast his orange glowing gaze downward. "It's her health. There's not a lot of time left for her and less breath. Her doctors are debating whether a set of artificial lungs would help or whether the shock to her system might be too much."

Dana took Kaylee by the hand. "I'm very sorry."

Snatching her hand away, Kaylee shot Charlie7 a scowl. "So, you brought Grammy Abby here to play stand-in? What were you thinking? Does Eve know about this?"

"Someone's probably informed her by now," Charlie7 admitted.

Kaylee threw up her hands. "I can't believe this! And you let her trade herself for me? Now who's supposed to negotiate with Ned?"

"She seemed intent on continuing in that role from the inside," Charlie7 explained. "It's non-standard, but for Abby, non-standard *is* standard."

Taking a heavy breath, Kaylee squared her shoulders and looked Charlie7 in the eye. "I demand that you go in there and save everyone. Ned might hesitate to kill the humans, but those poor robots are doomed. Someone needs to put a stop to this, and that's you."

Charlie7 twitched a sad smile. "You're like them, you know. Genetics and upbringing both; I suppose some similarity is inevitable. But Abby only pretends to order me around. Eve gets away with pretending a little more convincingly. But I don't take orders from anyone, especially not a young, freshly released hostage high on adrenaline."

"I'm forty-six!" Kaylee protested.

"I've had sneezes that lasted longer," Charlie7 replied flippantly. "But don't get in a snit. Abby passed me something just before embarking on this crazed scheme of hers. She said to give it to you. It's DNA encoded. I could crack it easily enough, but it'll be quicker if you do it."

Kaylee snatched the tiny sliver of a data crystal from his hands and borrowed a portable from Dana. Hers was still in the theater with Ned's gang. When Charlie7 attempted to follow her out the tent, she stabbed a finger in his direction. "Stay."

Pulling up short, the robot blinked.

"If there's anything you need to know, I'll share it with you. Since it's DNA encoded, it might be family business."

CHAPTER THIRTY-EIGHT

Kaylee's fingers shook as she sat on the seat of the washroom toilet with her pants up. It was the closest source of privacy she could find. The data crystal resisted her initial, clumsy attempts at insertion into the mayor's portable, but after a calming series of breaths, she tried again with better luck.

The DNA encoding was broken simply by having handled the crystal. The portable opened the message instantly.

"Kaylee, dear. I'm heading off to Mars in the next few minutes. I don't have long. If everyone else has gotten out safe and unharmed, I'm happy that my life was spent to some noble end. If the hostages are still in danger, and I've become one of them, I'm sorry. It's a crazy plan, I know, but it's the only one I've got, and if you're reading this and they're still captive, I must have tried swapping places with you. It was the only way I could think of to get you out of there without caving in to Ned Lund's wild demands.

"Kaylee, I need you. The backup plan is a last-ditch gambit. I promise I'll do whatever I can, but if I can't save everyone, I need you to get the only help that might. Under no circumstances are you to let Charlie7 handle negotiations or try some sort of damn fool heroics that could get everyone killed.

"Go to Earth. I'm enclosing coordinates. There's a reclusive old sack of servos who might be the only one with a solution. Say it was me who sent you.

"Good luck.

"Grammy Abby.

"P.S. I love you, and I wouldn't burden you with this if I didn't trust you to get the job done."

For a woman who only claimed to have a "few minutes" to leave final instructions, Grammy Abby had certainly filled up a page.

Taking liberties with Dana's portable, Kaylee punched in the coordinates left for her. They were for a tiny, remote island that hadn't been inhabited in her lifetime. There would be time for mysteries later.

Plucking the data crystal from her borrowed portable computer, Kaylee marched for the door, reconsidered, used the washroom unhurried for the first time in days, then swept out into the wider colony to confront a certain old robot.

"Charlie7," Kaylee called out. "We're leaving. Prep a spacero."

Charlie7 exited the tent, ducking under the flap with a shrewd look in his optic sensors. "What'd Abby tell you?"

"That you need to get me back to Earth on the double. She's going to do what she can, but we're the new backup plan."

She couldn't exactly tell Charlie7 that keeping him out of the Martian situation was a key part of that plan, but of all the intelligent creatures in the solar system, none had less grounds to complain about someone keeping secrets than Charlie7.

Less than twenty minutes later, a transport tech loaded Kaylee into a rapid-transit pod in the back of a spacero. She was a young woman, Martian-born and perky. She ran through a detailed list of warnings and precautions too quickly for Kaylee's harried mind to absorb. All too soon, she strapped Kaylee into place as the pod filled with a syrupy goo that might never come out of her clothing. It was a non-Newtonian G-shielding fluid that would allow Charlie7 to pilot the spacero as if he had a robotic passenger, not a fragile human one along.

The process had been more unpleasant than anything the Chain Breakers had done to her. Wires and probes stuck to her skin all over. A respiration mask covered Kaylee's nose and mouth, with tubes running down to her lungs, coated in an anesthetic film that kept her from gagging on them.

The transport tech pressed Kaylee's head back and packed it in place with foam blocks, including some weird devices that felt like suction cups over her eyes. "This is the worst part," the tech warned. "This is a hyper-oxygenated fluid. Don't try to breathe it. The pump will circulate it for you. I know... easier said than done. But the less you fight, it the more comfortable you'll be."

Blind and immobile, Kaylee fought back a wave of panic as the syrup flowed up over her chin, then into her ears, around the cups protecting her eyes. A muted thump must have been the pod door sealing shut over her.

She couldn't expand her lungs, the fluid pressure around her was like a sack of concrete on her chest. The thin trickle of air from the tubes was replaced by a sensation of drowning as fluid rushed in to fill her lungs.

Kaylee thrashed and tried to gasp, tried to cough it out. But the fluid and pod restraints held her motionless. She couldn't fight back against the liquid the pod pumped into her. Rationally, she knew it was for her protection, that she'd get all the oxygen she needed, regulated and metered with exacting precision. Yet her instincts forced her to struggle against the intrusions and alien sensations until she was too exhausted to resist.

There was no sensation from outside the pod. They'd warned her of the lack of communication between the pod and cockpit during transit. They'd also warned her that she couldn't be asleep because the life support system wasn't designed to safely regulate a comatose passenger. So she'd be stuck like this, quite literally, for hours.

And while everyone had assured her that, under these conditions, the trip from Mars to Earth could be made in a fraction of the time it normally would require, no one had told her that the trip would feel like years trapped motionless, drowning, and cut off from all sensory input.

CHAPTER THIRTY-NINE

Abby held her arms out to her sides and spun slowly on her heel. The cloth-o-matic garments were pleasantly warm, if devoid of style entirely. It was a worse torture for the poor machine than the theater's inhabitants likely faced, a costuming fabricator forced to produce the bland, colorless garments. She twisted her neck to check out her profile in the mirror.

"Didn't ask my measurements, and I doubt Mars has them on file," Abby said offhandedly. "That must mean I can still share clothes with my granddaughter."

"She filled it out better," Lester Saito remarked. Abby suspected he didn't realize she knew who he was or that she remembered him from before he emigrated to Mars. And if he had to watch a raisin-skinned version of Kaylee change clothes for "security reasons," it served him right. The ogling was worse for him than her, she assured herself.

"Well, you see how well eighty-one extra years sit on your bones," Abby said sharply.

At that point, Ned Lund reentered the room with that fellow Gregor at his side. "Damn clones," he muttered after a moment of studying her face. "Could've been I left Kaylee in here and she used the makeup kit."

Abby lifted her chin. "Collar away. I'm not the least bit frightened of you."

Ned shook his head. "First things first. We've got to be sure you're not concealing any tricky tech."

Abby arched an eyebrow, then titled her head toward Lester. "Ask this one. He watched me the whole time, though I imagine he better enjoyed leering at my granddaughter."

"You could have anything in you," Ned countered. He took a device from Gregor and approached. "We've got to wipe you to be sure."

Abby stiffened. "I assure you, I'm not my mother. I neither transmit nor receive data feeds." She tried to keep her breath from quickening, her pulse from racing. Backing up one step was as far as she got before Lester's firm hand rested against her back, blocking further retreat. "I do have a number of cybernetics that I rely on."

Ned walked up and jabbed a finger against her sternum. "Got a real, live heart in there?"

"Yes," Abby replied softly.

"Lungs?" he asked without removing his finger.

Abby nodded.

Ned tapped a finger against her forehead. "How about that brain of yours: synapses or crystal?"

"Biological," Abby replied.

"Hold her up," Ned ordered, and Lester hooked his hands under Abby's armpits.

Abby shut her eyes and held her breath.

The EMP machine clacked, the sudden pulse hitting her like a sledgehammer inside her own skull. They swept the device down her, disabling each and every technological upgrade that relied on electronics of any sort.

Abby's left arm was a limp collection of dead servos. Her hips and knees gave a whirring of forced motor action as her weight sagged into Lester's custody, unable to support her.

All along Abby's spine, magnetically floated artificial vertebrae now ground together like ill-fitting gears, sending glass-shard pain all up and down her back.

When she opened her eyes, the fully cybernetic implants conveyed no vision.

She heard the gasps without knowing who among them had been most horrified.

"Perhaps, this precaution went too far," Gregor suggested haltingly.

"Damn cyborg," Lester grunted in her ear. "Heavier than a little bird-boned thing like this should be. Give me a hand."

As rough hands took her ankles and lifted her from the floor, Abby reached across with her good hand and dragged her cybernetic arm across her body. The twisting motion of her spine was like forcing it through a meat grinder.

"Set her down in the seats," Ned ordered. "Damn, bloody robots. She's practically one of them."

"Oh, wouldn't that be nice," Abby remarked lightly through teeth clenched against the pain. Every bounce and jostle as two Neddites lugged her along was a fresh, searing stab wound. "Shut off all those annoying little malfunction errors. Not so lucky, though. But give me a few minutes to collect myself, and we can resume negotiations."

CHAPTER FORTY

Kaylee vomited.

It was her first reaction to breathing a mixture of air and silvery slime supposedly aerated to sustain her better than the real thing. The shower at Franklin Hospital poured warm water over her, rinsing the gels and fluids down the floor drain as she coughed on hands and knees, trying to acclimate herself amid sensations of vertigo and a burning down her throat and trachea.

The delay felt like an indulgence. But Charlie7 hadn't needed to know the details of the plan just yet. Set it in motion, get too far, then allow him in on the scheme. That was Kaylee's plan.

Yet for all she knew, Mars had turned into a graveyard, and Alan was dead. And here she was, shivering and puking beneath a waterfall of pure, clean water.

"No rush," Charlie7 said from the doorway, voice echoing on the tile interior walls. "You're no good to anyone until you pull yourself together."

Pull yourself together, she echoed in her mind. That was the only task worth focusing on just then.

Kaylee took long, slow breaths, punctuated by occasional coughing as she emptied the last of the nutrient medium from her lungs. "Why isn't this a more popular way to travel?" she croaked.

Charlie7's chuckle answered first. "They hadn't used that rig in years. Hardly anyone's ever in enough of a hurry. These days, your kind is more likely to stretch the trip out and make it a week in relative comfort."

Short of breath and clawing her way to a nearby towel, Kaylee dragged herself from beneath the shower flow. She dressed in spare clothes that someone had conveniently commed ahead for her. Suspiciously, the outfit was a favorite from her Earth years and only programmed into her cloth-o-matic back at her old home in Paris.

She exited the shower room fully dressed and drying the last of the water from her hair. Kaylee's innards felt scraped clean—the raw, pink sort of clean that had removed a layer of skin but clean nonetheless. She needed a meal, a beer, and a half-day trip to a spa.

Kaylee settled for getting back to her task. "Where's the landing pad?"

"I think you need a stop first," Charlie7 said with surprising tenderness in his voice. He led Kaylee down a short corridor to a room reserved for a single VIP patient.

Great-Grammy Eve was a ghost of herself. Hooked up to tubes and wires, her every vital system was summed up in graphs and data dumps spread across a dozen screens around the room, all carefully out of the patient's field of view. A rhythmic hiss of forced, mechanical breathing brought back a vivid reminder of Kaylee's own recent adventure.

Imagine not being able to escape to breathe on her own at the conclusion of the trip. Kaylee suppressed a shudder for her great-grandmother's sake.

"Oh, look," a voice modulator tucked at Eve's side said in her voice. "Another visitor. Had I known dying would make me so popular, I'd have tried it years ago."

Kaylee donned a smile and came over to her great-grandmother's side. "I came from Mars just now. Sorry if I'm a little bedraggled."

Eve raised one eyebrow a twitch. "You. Bedraggled? I can imagine what I must look like then. Is there a word far enough below bedraggled?"

"For 148, you look great," Kaylee said.

"Historically," Eve said via the box, "148 years looked like two dates and a name listed on a stone marker."

"I'd like to stay longer," Kaylee said with a pang in her stomach unrelated to hunger. "But I have work to do to help the hostages on Mars."

"I'm aware," Eve replied. She blinked her eyes rapidly to draw attention to them. "I can see the news feeds, still. Damn fool daughter of mine."

"You'll see Grammy Abby again," Kaylee said. "I promise."

"Don't make promises you know you can't keep," Eve admonished, still great-grandmothering from her hospital bed. "Reputations are more valuable than comforting lies."

"I'll try to remember," Kaylee said with a wink before ducking out the door.

"If you have a plan you'd like to share, I'm all ears," Charlie7 said. "It'll have to be a quick one if you have any intention of keeping that promise. I know Abby's not going to put up with traveling the way you just did."

"I need to borrow your spacero," Kaylee said.

"I really hate that term," Charlie7 replied. "Where are we going?"

"Just me," Kaylee said. "I'll keep it under 7-G and try not to scratch the paint. Nothing out of atmosphere; I just need the closest ride."

"Mind telling me what's going on?"

"Yes."

Charlie7 snorted a chuckle. "OK. I'll play along. But I'm going to want answers soon."

Kaylee handed back the DNA-encoded chip. "Eve has the right DNA. There's a message for her too. Watch it together."

And with that, Kaylee was off. She tore through the hospital, dodging staff and equipment in the halls. When she reached Charlie7's spacero, she dodged around the transport pod, still dripping gel on the concrete where they'd extracted her, and hopped in.

Her destination, provided by her grandmother, was a tiny island in the South Pacific by the name of Rapa Nui—also known as Easter Island.

CHAPTER FORTY-ONE

As a rule, Abby abhorred vandalism. Today, she was feeling charitable. Her vandals admitted their acts, even asked her approval. It wasn't that the theater chairs were naturally uncomfortable, it was just that she was in no fit shape to use them as the theater designer intended them.

Thus it was that Abby Fourteen reclined in a fold-down seat with the chair in front of her torn from its moorings and flipped around to act as a makeshift ottoman. It wobbled precariously if she shifted in her seat, but as each movement was an agonized grating of scrap metal in practically every joint in her body, Abby was inclined to keep still.

The collar had been a mild indignity by comparison. Explosively separating her shoulders from her head at least would have put an end to the pain.

Not that she would give Ned Lund and his cronies the satisfaction.

The other hostages cooed over her like first-time parents over a sick newborn.

"Is that comfortable?"

"How about now?"

"Are you hungry?"

"Let me get that for you."

She let them nursemaid her, knowing that it kept their mind off their own predicament. However, she wasn't at the Arthur Miller Theater on holiday.

"Can I get you anything?" one of them asked.

"Yes," Abby replied. "Ned Lund."

There was a squeamish silence. Then one of her fellow hostages suggested, "Maybe that's not a good idea, considering your condition."

"I just want to talk to him, not arm wrestle," Abby replied briskly.

One of her nannies departed, bare feet slapping the floor as he headed off. Truth be told, she had a headache fit to split firewood. The sooner she said her piece to Ned, the sooner she might nod off and regain some of her strength.

Her breath wheezed through a bronchial filter that was no longer self-cleaning.

"What's up?" Wil asked. She'd never gotten a good look at the other hostages, but she'd made a point of learning her captors by voice. "Whatever you need Ned for, I'll take care of."

"Can you authorize a surrender and peaceful release of all these hostages?" Abby asked glibly. Keeping a disaffected air took a force of will when each breath came through a wet cloth in her bronchial tubes and even the movement of her jaw muscles jostled the grating vertebrae in her neck.

"Come off it, lady," Wil replied. "If you want us to get a doctor in here, maybe I can—"

Abby held up her good hand. "No. I'm fine. Nothing a doctor could do without equipment I doubt you'd let her bring. I'm just ready to restart negotiations for Ned's list of demands."

"Look, you're stuck in here," Wil pointed out. "Nobody out there's going to honor any agreement you make."

"Why ever not?" Abby asked. "That's why I'm in here. They know it out there. None of *them* are going to talk to you unless someone patches you through to my mother. Believe me, that's one outcome you don't want."

"Why not?" Wil asked. "Eve Fourteen can move mountains. We just about need that."

"I need you to believe me," Abby said. "I'm your last chance. I don't want anything but all these nice people going home safely, robots included."

Wil grunted. "Yeah, figures you're soft on them. Bunch of bossy freeloaders have puffed you and yours up plenty."

"Sorry, I've lost track," Abby said. "Aren't the bossy freeloaders the ones with bombs, getting their meals delivered and making demands?"

"The robots, smart-ass," Wil snapped.

"Manners, young man. I'd like to say we had them in my day, but this is still my day and we clearly haven't. Not that it's been pleasant talking to you, but I must cut our discourse short. The mind is willing to joust at windmills for the pleasure of it, but the lungs demand a brief rest. Send Ned over, but don't rush on my account."

The longer he took, the better. Abby could use the rest, and stalling was a more profitable use of her time than butting heads with an ox like Ned. If she pulled out a miraculous agreement, so be it, but keeping Ned occupied and not murdering innocent robots was a worthwhile end in and of itself.

"Crazy old biddy," Wil muttered as he stalked off in the direction of the stage.

Abby didn't let on that there was neither anything cybernetic nor faulty about her hearing. She kept her eyes shut to stave off the feeling of blindness brought on by having open lids and nothing to see. Resting her head against the low back of her chair was only possible thanks to the improvised footrest, for which she was increasingly grateful.

There were times when vandalism could be an act of kindness.

CHAPTER FORTY-TWO

harlie7's spacero was a piece of work. It had more custom modifications than any vehicle Kaylee had ever ridden in, let alone piloted. A spacero was really just a skyro that had come off the assembly line utterly perfect down to the microcrystalline structure of the hull. The Kanto robots then pulled it aside and fitted it for space travel instead of mere atmospheric flight.

Extreme speeds.

Extreme forces.

Vast distances with no help for millions of kilometers.

Most spacero owners didn't mess with them at all and left even the most basic maintenance tasks to the manufacturers. But most robots didn't possess the blinding arrogance and positively reinforced self-assurance of Charlie7. Strike that; none came close.

Kaylee had to browse unfamiliar, additional consoles with functions she dared not delve into before finding all the avionics controls she needed. The setup was altered to better fit the oversized Version 70.2 that had practically become Charlie7's trademark—which coincidentally made it harder for the slightly undersized Madison chassis that Kaylee wore.

Still, autopilot did most of the work. No doubt, the stool pigeon machine had reported her destination to its owner. Charlie7 would have no trouble figuring out Kaylee's plan.

It occurred to her that the wily old robot probably had a better idea what she might find there than she did. Perhaps a quick comm might...

No. Stick to the plan.

Whatever was on Rapa Nui, Grammy Abby trusted Kaylee to figure it out on her own.

With clouds shooting past the cockpit window like bullets, Kaylee relaxed and took a nap. She needed to quiet her mind and prepare herself for whatever surprise might lay ahead of her.

She jolted awake when the autopilot touched down with a rough thump.

Kaylee hadn't meant to sleep the *whole* trip away. She'd wanted to plan, to maybe check the Solarwide for clues as to the significance of this location. It used to house a medical sanctuary back in the days of illegal human cloning. She shuddered to think what might still be left behind that could aid the release of hostages on another planet.

Was one of Ned's genetic twins buried here? Impossible. He was natural born.

Could there be an old computer system, one not hooked into the Solarwide, containing incriminating evidence? Possibly, but Grammy Abby might have overestimated Kaylee's skills with old computer systems if that were the case.

"Hello?" someone called out. "Is anyone in there?" There was a knocking at the spacero's hull.

Scrambling to hit the cockpit release, Kaylee straightened in her seat and wiped a line of drool from her lips with the back of her hand. "Sorry. Yes. Me. Must have dozed off with the autopilot engaged."

Climbing out of the spacero, she saw that her host was a younger woman, blonde, wearing a pale seafoam uniform and carrying a portable computer.

"I already know you don't have an appointment," the woman said with a nonthreatening smile that looked professionally practiced. "But do you have a referral by any chance?"

"Referral?" Kaylee echoed. She peered past the seafoam woman to a commune of whitewashed stone buildings with red clay tile roofs half a kilometer down a hillside trail. "I don't have a... what is this place?"

The woman knit her brow and tilted her head to one side. "This is the Neurological Recovery Retreat. We provide discreet neurological diagnoses and treatment advice to a select group of patients. We comply with all Human Welfare Committee guidance. Can I ask why you're here?"

Kaylee squirmed her outfit into a more comfortable position, but there would be no comfort under that judging gaze. "I... well... my grandmother suggested I might find what I was looking for here. My name is—"

"Kaylee Fourteen," the woman replied with a smile. "Sorry. Must get tiresome. But there are only so many Madison clones. You're too young to be Wendy and too old by far to be Athena."

"Athena is natural born," Kaylee said defensively. It didn't help that the girl *still* looked just like her, but Alan had an equal share of the girl's genetic history.

"Of course," the woman in seafoam replied. "My mistake. If you'll come this way, the director will see you immediately. Abby Fourteen doesn't send many patients this way."

Kaylee fell in behind the seafoam uniform as her guide set a brisk pace. "Wait. I'm not a patient."

"Technically, no one is," the woman replied without looking back. "While we do maintain the highest standards in diagnostics and advice, we don't perform any treatments on site. Any and all follow-up will be coordinated with your regular therapist."

"I don't *have* a therapist," Kaylee insisted.

The woman turned without slowing. "We can help you find one. If Abby Fourteen thought you needed to see us, I'm sure the director will make sure you're not left adrift in want of follow-up treatment."

Kaylee slowed. "What's your name?"

The other woman stopped. "Oh, I'm sorry. I'm Megan Mengele, assistant neurologist at head of patient relations."

"Well, Megan, can you explain why my grandmother might have sent me here?"

Megan appeared taken aback. "I know we're remote here, but we still have Solarwide access. We've seen the news. Frankly, I'm not surprised that your grandmother's first worry about you was making sure you got checked out for psychological trauma."

When Megan resumed her walk, Kaylee stayed rooted in place.

The data crystal. The harrowing ride packed up in nauseating, G-dampening goo. The mysterious errand. Was it all a ruse to get Kaylee back to Earth in time to visit with Grammy Eve one last time and get help for post-traumatic neurological harm?

Grammy Abby had gone to these incredible lengths, making Kaylee feel like the linchpin of some grand scheme, just to send her to a secret, unlicensed therapist.

Momentum and curiosity combined to carry her onward at a shuffling pace. Megan slowed to match.

When they entered the main building, the old world facades were replaced by ultra-modern styling. Everything was sleek, black or silver, glossy, and most of the walls doubled as video screens. The doors were enormous, large enough that Grampa Plato could have walked through with his arms outstretched either to his sides or overhead without touching.

Each door opened with a quiet shush upon their approach. Thick carpets quieted their footsteps. A scent of lavender carried in the air, making the cold stylings less intimidating and more elegant.

"Just have a seat. The director will be along in a moment."

Megan swept her hand toward the room beyond the next door. Kaylee pulled up short. There were regular office chairs—with legs, not wheels or magnetic floaters—but one option for sitting caught Kaylee's breath in her throat.

The elaborate chair at the far side of the room was padded in black leather, including the heavy armrests and leg rests. It reclined, supported on a single metallic pillar under the back. At the head, a webwork of steel bands, probes, and wires surrounded an area the size and shape of a human head. It poised above the U-shaped headrest like a spider ready to strike.

"One of the regular chairs is fine," Megan prompted.

Kaylee stepped hesitantly inside, and the door slid shut behind her. Part of her wanted to turn around and make sure she could open it once more. Another part warned that if she wanted answers to why Grammy Abby had sent her here, knowing *that* answer might derail her train of thought.

Instead, Kaylee crossed the room and inspected what she could only imagine was a scanning machine. Everything Megan claimed would have been a lie if the device was a human upload rig like the one from the old documentaries.

Kaylee's mother claimed to have viewed Evelyn11's work, the experiments that had eventually resulted in all the Madison Maxwell-Chang clones existing. Kaylee had lived in that lab, after a fashion, as a cluster of pre-embryonic cells, but that hardly counted. At her mother's advice, she'd never watched the damning evidence of the Eves before her great-grandmother.

But everyone knew generally that the equipment resembled a robotic upload bed.

Hearing her own breathing in the quiet confines of the medical office, Kaylee crouched beside the scanner's chair and peered underneath.

Behind her, the door shushed open.

"If you're looking for straps, there aren't any," a synthetic voice replied with the cadence and faint accent of an Evelyn-mixed robot.

Kaylee stiffened. She didn't want to look back but felt compelled.

Gemini was a footnote, a relic of history long forgotten by polite society. Kaylee had never met her, had rarely had the name cross her mind in her life. But the instant she saw the creature in the doorway, that name sprang instantly to mind.

In the face, there was an understandable yet vague resemblance to Grampa Plato. But that face hung slack, held up by straps and clamps and screws. Even the eyelids were propped by tiny servo arms, revealing those piercing irises that focused in Kaylee's direction. The rest of the body was a scaffolding of robotic components scattered around withered flesh that it dragged into the room as an accessory.

"I'll allow you your moment of gawking like a pufferfish," Gemini said, though the voice came from an emitter at her throat. "Everyone needs a certain amount of it, it seems. Best to get it out of the way all at once up front."

Kaylee didn't know quite what to say. This creature was a monstrosity, inside and out. She'd been the robot who tried to turn Eve clones into vessels for her robotic intellect, raising them like cattle, training their mental faculties in the hope of producing a brain complex enough to fit her vast consciousness. And now she was little more than a human mind in a robotic body. There didn't appear to be any function at all to her flesh. Bare, naked flesh hung limp, pinioned to an exoskeleton that did all the work. Just enough of her skin was covered to pass decency monitoring for the pre-emancipated, yet she was still somehow an obscenity.

"Had enough yet?" Gemini asked.

"I'm sorry," Kaylee said, covering her mouth. "I'm just—"

"No. Go on. Continue. Clearly not."

Kaylee swallowed. "I... I don't know why my grandmother sent me here."

"Psychological shock, you're guessing. In an Eve?" Gemini scoffed, a grating sound in artificial modulation. "Those minds of yours are made of granite."

Kaylee spasmed a quick smile. "Yours must be too."

"What? This body?" Gemini asked. "I suffer less than you imagine. Most of my neural inputs are blocked off. Nuisances, mainly. The greatest inconvenience I suffer is sleep. Other than that, it's almost like being a clumsy, fool spectacle of a robot. But that's not the point. *Why* are you here?"

"I was hoping you might tell me," Kaylee countered. She couldn't help it if her eyes strayed to Gemini's bald scalp, where metallic spikes drove directly into her skull, connecting to what appeared to be a computer at the back of her head.

"You say Abbigail sent you?"

Kaylee nodded. "You knew her?"

"She came to me for questions the psychiatrists wouldn't answer—couldn't answer. I understand the brain, but I'm not allowed to treat human patients. There are a few neurologists who use my scans, though most won't admit it in academic circles. Abby liked knowing that her brain was getting the proper attention."

"Could there be something hidden in my brain?" Kaylee guessed.

"I'd be happy to scan you," Gemini replied with a shrug of servo motors that lifted her limp human shoulders. "Completely non-invasive. Far more accurate than the old systems you might have seen in the archives. But I don't imagine who'd have put a message in there."

"Then I can't really see why Grammy Abby would send me here."

Gemini chuckled electronically. "Grammy Abby... my dear child, however you were raised, you're all sisters. These honorifics get more convoluted with each generation. But why *did* Abbigail send you?"

"She wanted me off Mars?"

"Too facile an answer. You were safe anywhere outside that miserable theater. Why is Abbigail there in the first place? Why not anyone else?"

"She was the first choice as negotiator after Gra—after Eve." She didn't want the fact that the Fourteen family tree was more of a lawn interfering with her more relevant points.

"Is she a fit substitute?" Gemini asked. "Who here on Earth might have done better?"

Kaylee wracked her brain. There were brilliant minds scattered all across Earth—and Mars, too, for that matter. But there were few who could bring the sort of gravitas and air of authority that Abby carried. Any robot would have been instantly ruled out as a negotiator, being a hostile target of Ned Lund's whole worldview.

"Short of Charlie7 arguing with a magnetic pistol? No one."

Gemini raised a mechanical finger. Its fleshy counterpart remaining limp somewhere near the robotic wrist. "Ah. No one but Eve."

Kaylee shook her head. "That's a non-starter. There's no way she could survive the trip. She's barely surviving a hospital bed." The mere thought of her great-grandmother's last moments had Kaylee wiping a tear from her eye.

The flesh at Gemini's lips pulled back a hair, showing off yellowed teeth. "Aha. There is one way she could make the trip—make it easily and comfortably, no less."

"Some sort of relay?" Kaylee asked, eying the scanning rig. "A robotic surrogate."

Gemini rocked back on her heels. "Possibly, though I doubt that Neddite clod would accept such a clunky system. No. I have a portable rig. It's slower than the one in the room with us but no less accurate."

Kaylee scowled. "If you don't think the relay would work, then... no. No way. Eve Fourteen would *never* upload to a robotic body. It would go against everything she stands for."

"Everything?" Gemini asked. "Even saving the life of her only daughter?"

Kaylee's mouth went dry. "Grammy Abby's 127."

"And I'm 145. These are no longer the Dark Ages. Life is limited in length only by the technology we wish to apply to it. Abbigail might live another hundred years or another thousand. And whether the two of them are sisters in reality, Eve still thinks of her as a daughter."

Grammy Abby couldn't possibly have been this cold-blooded. Could she? But Kaylee couldn't see another solution. Then again, there was one hitch with this plan that perhaps Gemini didn't see. "But she'd be a robot. Ned Lund wouldn't negotiate with her."

Gemini snorted—more of an electronic blat than a proper noise. "She'd still be Eve Fourteen. There was always something special about that one."

The jigsaw puzzle was complete on the table before her, and Kaylee was refusing to look down to see what image it showed. Abbigail Fourteen had played the only gambit she could think of. Eve *was* the only one who could credibly give in to all Ned Lund's demands. Eve's word carried committee authority. Her grandmother had counted on a mother's love to twist Eve's arm into doing the unthinkable.

Kaylee gritted her teeth and held out a hand. "Give me the portable rig."

"I've already dispatched Megan to fetch it. She's loading it into your vessel."

Gemini followed as Kaylee headed back to Charlie7's spacero.

"This is going to open a floodgate, isn't it?" Kaylee asked. "Eve Fourteen can't accept this bargain without allowing others. Is that your reason for helping?"

"It may surprise you to learn that I'd assist you in whatever ways possible, regardless of my personal circumstances," Gemini replied. "If you'd arrived and realized that the horrors of captivity were foremost on your mind, I'd have scanned your brain and sent you off with an excellent recommendation for a therapist."

"But you'll take a robotic body if it's available, won't you?"

Gemini shrugged.

Megan was finished loading the scanning rig into the back of the spacero—the spot most recently occupied by the G-shielded transport pod—by the time Kaylee and Gemini arrived.

Climbing into the cockpit, Kaylee paused halfway. "Anything I should know about how to work it?"

"Don't," Gemini advised. "You'll need help from Kanto to find her some chassis or another. Charlie13 ought to have no trouble operating it."

"What about Charlie7?" Kaylee asked. There was always the chance that Kanto might prove unhelpful. There were agendas and hidden politics galore within the cavernous factory. It had a higher population than Mars all by itself.

"Charlie7 knows what every person on this planet had for breakfast this morning," Gemini said in a gravelly snarl unmistakable even in synthetic mimicry.

"I'll take that as a yes," Kaylee said as she closed the canopy.

Hitting the throttle, she set a course for Human Era Japan, home of the ancient factory that grew to become Kanto. Once comfortably airborne, she sent a message to Charlie7.

"I don't care how. Get Eve to Kanto. Figure something out."

The last thing she sent him was an image from the spacero's cargo cubby. But if Charlie7 was the robot everyone claimed, she suspected...

ALREADY HALFWAY THERE.

...he already knew.

CHAPTER FORTY-THREE

Shortly after Kaylee departed from Philadelphia in his spaceroamer, Charlie7 found himself commiserating with the generation wedged in between. Wendy and Lucas had shipped their grandchildren back to Oxford but remained in the city out of familial duty. Charlie7 caught up with them in a coffee shop just a block from the hospital.

"Hey, Gramps," Lucas had greeted him upon entry, toasting with a steaming ceramic cup in hand.

"Charlie7, come on over. Share a table," Wendy had added.

He indulged them in stories about a younger Eve's exploits, regaling them with tales told and retold in fiction and performances on stage and screen. No human of the current age was so well documented, but they couldn't get enough of Charlie7's perspective.

Lucas shook his head, looking down into his cup. "I can't imagine this world without her. It's like a continent is dying."

"A monument, at least," Wendy said. "You almost get the feeling that the second she breathes her last, the Earth's going to sag on one side for lack of her holding it up."

He thought back to the video he'd just watched with Eve. It was a series of videos, actually, recorded over the years, in which Abby began by apologizing—time after time—for the stupid thing she'd presumably done to get herself killed. Eve had cried through the whole of it, realizing that for every precautionary recording Abby had made over the years, this time she truly believed she wasn't going to see her mother again.

After that, Eve had wanted to be alone. The hospital had orders to alert the family if her condition deteriorated. If Charlie7 wanted the latest news—without hacking into the hospital staff's accounts— sitting around telling stories to her granddaughter and his own grandson seemed like the way to pass the time.

Kaylee hadn't given him everything. The data crystal had been altered—quite expertly, to his dismay—to excise Abby's instructions to the girl.

He couldn't leave Kaylee and whatever plans lay between her and Abby to meander unsupervised. If there was one thing that Earth had shown him, time and again, it was that the planet couldn't get by without him. Mars wasn't looking to do much better.

He accessed the root-level override codes for his spaceroamer and checked its heading.

Easter Island.

Abby had sent Kaylee to Easter Island for some reason. Charlie7 was well acquainted with the work that went on at the facility—far better acquainted than the regulators who dropped in for periodic inspections. Only two humans lived there, and one of those two barely fit the most liberal definition.

As Charlie7 blathered on about Eve's brief time as honorary starter of the Paris Marathon, the bulk of his quantum gate operations went to solving the mystery of why.

Gemini was the foremost expert on the human mind. Her illicit study of the Eve clones was still the most in-depth study of cognitive mapping, and she'd developed her scanning methods into a non-invasive version that satisfied the Human Welfare Committee's strict guidelines for testing and study of the human brain.

He could see only two reasons for Abby to ship Kaylee off to Easter Island in such a rush. Both of them required Eve's brain. Both of them would require a robotic chassis. The only variance between the two plans would be whether Abby intended for Kaylee to get Eve to Mars as a robot or as a robotic impostor.

Kaylee was heading to Easter Island to pick up a scanning rig.

"What made her think she could win one at age sixty?" Lucas asked, shaking his head.

"You know grandma," Wendy said with a chuckle. "Never thinks she's going to lose. Came in eighth out of ten runners, and she called it a moral victory."

Charlie7 chuckled along at the right point to imply they had his full attention.

A key piece of the puzzle was missing. Why would Eve go along with it?

Oh, dear.

She hadn't.

Had she?

Had Abby thrown herself on the tracks of a runaway train just to force Eve into action? Fond as she might have been of Kaylee, Athena, Stephen, or any number of nieces, nephews, and assorted relations by marriage, she only had one daughter. Plato was long dead. Eve had outlived her sisters one by one. With her own life dangling by a thread of modern medical science, could Eve knowingly let Abby remain in the hands of a madman?

The irrational, impetuous actions of a playwright out of her league now suddenly made perfect—if still crazed—sense. Abby could write plays about hostage negotiations from now until the heat death of the universe, but that wouldn't qualify her to do the job when lives were on the line. Eve was built for hard decisions, for dealing with stubborn, pig-headed robots.

"Excuse me," Charlie7 said, pushing back his chair. "I have something to take care of."

Wendy waved. "Don't go far. We'll let you know if we hear anything."

"Don't be a stranger," Lucas admonished.

As soon as he was out of the coffee shop's line of sight, Charlie7 burst into a run. Fleet as he was afoot, he was faster worming his way into Franklin Hospital's computer systems. A quick shift of duty assignments cleared a path. A false feedback loop kept the security systems from recording his passage. He recorded Eve's vital signs, designed an algorithm to simulate natural variance, and fed it back into the monitors hooked to her.

On the hospital roof, a medevac skyroamer powered up its engines unattended.

Charlie7 stalked down a deserted hallway on the hospital's third floor, making a beeline for Eve's room. Her eyelids fluttered at his entry.

"Don't mind me," Charlie7 said. "Get some sleep. We're just going for a little ride."

"A ride?" the voice box on her bedside table squawked. "Where?"

Charlie7 unplugged the box.

"You've got more old friends to see," he told her. "Text if you need to talk. It doesn't bother me the way it does the humans."

He pushed Eve's bed down the hall, breathing pump slung over his shoulder with an umbilical drawing power from a port in his abdomen.

A quick lift ride to the roof and Charlie7 enacted a reverse sort of medical evac flight. He loaded his patient gingerly into the secure pod on the side, reconnecting the life support apparatus to the vessel's power.

THIS HAD BETTER NOT BE ANOTHER OF YOUR CRAZY SCHEMES.

"It's not," Charlie7 reassured her aloud. That much was true, if not plainly so. This was clearly either Abby or Kaylee's crazy plan; he was just going along with it.

DESPITE THE CLICHÉ, I FEEL COMPELLED TO POINT OUT THAT I'M TOO OLD FOR THIS.

"I've never found age to be a limiting factor."

EASY FOR A ROBOT TO SAY.

Charlie7 bit his tongue. "C'mon. Take it easy. Hey, I can promise you there won't be any annoying doctor's visits the whole ride."

FINE. LAST ONE. TOO TIRED TO ARGUE RIGHT NOW. BETTER MAKE IT GOOD.

By the time Kaylee's message arrived, Charlie7 was already over the Pacific Ocean.

I DON'T CARE HOW. GET EVE TO KANTO. FIGURE SOMETHING OUT.

"Already halfway there," he text messaged back with a smug grin on his face.

He wondered whether anyone would ever make a documentary about *his* life. No one ever seemed to appreciate how much more smoothly the world worked with him in it.

Hours later, as they neared their destination, Eve's vital signs sped. Charlie7 had been monitoring them the whole way. She'd dozed off somewhere over the Rocky Mountains. Now, she'd awakened.

WHERE ARE WE?

"Can't you tell by the constellations?" Charlie7 asked.

I WAS ATTEMPTING TO BE POLITE. WHY THE HELL ARE WE HEADING TO KANTO? AND WHY ARE LONG-RANGE COMMUNICATIONS JAMMED?

"I apologize for everything," Charlie7 messaged back.

THAT DIDN'T ANSWER A SINGLE QUESTION.

"You are correct. It didn't."

CHAPTER FORTY-FOUR

Kaylee paced the rooftop landing zone of Kanto's Southeast Region-5 like a bank robber waiting for her getaway driver to show up. That the skyro she'd flown clearly belonged to someone else and the scanning rig in the back of it was at best a morally gray piece of contraband weren't helping her peace of mind.

Charlie7 had declined to provide an arrival time—or any follow-ups to her queries at all.

On her portable, Kaylee checked the news feeds. There was a minor uproar in committee circles over the Neddite hostage takers getting access codes for a pair of mining ships working the Kuiper Belt. Questions swirled over who authorized the transfer of command, why the negotiating team made the deal, and whether the Neddites would even honor it.

But there was no sign that anyone on Mars had been hurt—robot or human—and there was no manhunt for a missing Eve. Kaylee didn't even want to know how Charlie7 had managed that.

No one had contacted Kaylee about her presence on the roof. She'd chosen a low-traffic landing zone on purpose. Workers inside the factory seemed either oblivious to or dismissive of her being there.

"Come on, you rusted pile of ancient circuitry," Kaylee muttered to herself. "Where are you?"

As she scanned the horizon to the east, she saw a blip. At first, she worried it might just be another bird, but this bird grew too fast, its approach too obviously rapid, for it to be any creature.

The skyro with Charlie7 and Eve drew near. Kaylee rushed to the spacero to relay her landing coordinates before pulling up short. Of course, Charlie7 knew where she was. It was his spacero. No doubt he'd been tracking her since she left.

At times, Kaylee wondered what it must be like to have that duality of existence, living and yet being so tied into technology that it became second nature. She made a mental note to ask her great-grandmother if this all came together.

When the medevac skyro with its white and red exterior came in for its final approach, Kaylee shielded her face against the blowback from the engines. As soon as the engines powered down, she rushed to the occupied patient transport pod.

Kaylee popped the canopy of the pod. "Eve? Grammy? Are you all right?"

Eve opened her eyes a squint. There was no response.

Then Kaylee heard a chime from her portable.

KAYLEE, WHAT ARE YOU DOING HERE? DID ALL OF
PHILADELPHIA RELOCATE?

She wiped worried tears from her eyes. "It's a long story. I'll tell it on the way."

Charlie7 came around and took custody of both the portable upload rig and Eve's gurney—including the portable life support pump. Kaylee fell in behind as the robot navigated their way into the labyrinthine depths of the factory. She kept her portable out to converse with Eve.

"Alan got caught up trying to be a hero, working to stamp out the Human First movement on Mars. He infiltrated the Chain Breakers and got himself caught as a spy. When I went to visit my Unity Keeper friends, I—"

NEWS FEEDS COVERED THIS. SKIP TO WHY WE'RE
HERE.

"I'm explaining!" Kaylee protested, though she could hardly begrudge a dying woman her impatience. There was still a chance that she wouldn't even survive the trip through the factory.

THIS PLACE BRINGS BACK SO MANY MEMORIES...

"Well, since you weren't available to negotiate the hostage standoff—which everyone agreed you were the only one qualified for—Grammy Abby decided to give it a try. Turns out, she never figured on brokering a deal. She was there to buy time... and one other thing."

WHAT OTHER THING?

Kaylee choked up before she could force the word out. "She's there to die instead of me. Trading places with me was the best she thought she could do. She had a backup plan and only one backup plan that might save her and the others."

DAMN YOU BOTH. I SHOULD HAVE SEEN THIS
COMING. TAKE ADVANTAGE OF AN OLD WOMAN'S
FEEBLEMINDEDNESS, WHY DON'T YOU?

"You're not feebleminded," Charlie7 said, showing for the first time that he was either peeking at Kaylee's portable or she needed to update her security protocols. "You're feeble-bodied."

"And you could go to Mars and talk sense into those Chain Breaker idiots," Kaylee added. "But you'd need a body that can survive the trip."

I'M NOT A HYPOCRITE.

"No one would say that you are, given the circumstances," Charlie7 replied. "I'm also fine with taking the fall for forcing you to go through with it."

ARE YOU FORCING ME?

"Grammy Abby is," Kaylee said. "It's still your decision. But how can you not try to save her?"

Eve closed her eyes.

IT'S AGAINST COMMITTEE EDICTS. NO HUMAN UPLOAD
TO CRYSTALLINE MATRIX BRAINS. NOT VOLUNTARY,
NOT OTHERWISE.

"The vote's been locked at 8-7 for decades," Charlie7 countered.

Kaylee quickly punched up a login screen for the Human Welfare Committee member portal. "Thumb print would be all it takes," she said. "Change your vote. Go to Mars. You'll fix everything."

Eve remained silent.

Two sets of footsteps clanged on the metallic floors of the factory catwalks. The breathing pump hissed in and out. Kaylee looked to Charlie7 for reassurance, to check that Eve wasn't slipping away on them. The robot winked in reply.

IT WAS THE HEBREWS WHO NAMED THE FIRST WOMAN
EVE. IN GREEK MYTH, I WOULD HAVE BEEN CALLED
PANDORA. MORE APPROPRIATE, I THINK, GIVEN THE
BOX I PONDER OPENING.

"That box contained death," Charlie7 pointed out, saving Kaylee from dredging up old school lessons for a counter argument. "This one contains the cure."

I WON'T LET ANYONE ELSE BE PRESSURED INTO
THIS.

"You'd still be around to ensure everyone's rights get looked after," Kaylee said.

I HAVE EVERY RIGHT TO SELF-TERMINATE ONCE ABBY
AND THE OTHERS ARE SAFE.

"I haven't regretted my choice in eleven and a half centuries," Charlie7 replied.

I'M ONLY DOING THIS BECAUSE OF DIRE NEED AND
THE UTTER INCOMPETENCE OF MY DAUGHTER, THE
MARTIAN AUTHORITIES, AND EVERY OTHER WOULD-BE
VOICE OF HUMANITY.

"And we'll make sure they're all ashamed of themselves," Kaylee promised.

"It's either that or hope their martyrdom creates a backlash that quells the Humans First movement for a few years," Charlie7 said with a shrug that jostled Eve's bed.

FINE. GIVE ME THAT THUMB SCANNER.

With a few additional touches of the screen, Eve brought up the standing committee vote on voluntary human-to-robot upload. She pressed her thumb to the screen and the header changed from FAILED to PASSED.

Once done, Eve closed her eyes once more.

WAKE ME WHEN IT'S TIME.

CHAPTER FORTY-FIVE

Abby hummed softly to herself. It wasn't any tune she knew but rather one she was developing. The minor key melody suited the dreary mood of the prison theater and might form the kernel of a showtune for an eventual stage adaptation.

She shook her head slightly, laughing silently at her own pretension. Abby wasn't even certain of escaping this standoff with her life. She'd strung Ned along, and he'd shown a remarkable reluctance to short-circuit the negotiations. The motion of her neck hurt but less than it ought to have.

Abby suspected that someone had been dosing her food with anti-inflammatory drugs.

The clop of hard-soled boots, combined with the particular gait she'd come to recognize, signaled the approach of the Chain Breakers' leader.

"You talk to them," Ned said, taking Abby's hand and pressing a portable into it. "Tell them what you promised me."

With a sigh, Abby obliged. "Send the native Martian children back, Dana. Of all the items on the list of demands, that one seems easiest."

"We can't just ship children around the solar system like commodities," Dana protested. *"They're children."*

"Get signed permission from the parents. Of the hostages in here, Dawn Cafferty and Fatima Sharif both consent. You handle the rest."

"That consent is under duress."

"It's all under duress," Abby replied. "We're still doing it." She fumbled around until she found the spot on the touch screen to shut off the call.

Ned took back custody of the portable. "She's got another hour."

"And then you'll start murdering people," Abby added.

"Not people," Ned said. "Robots." Then he stalked away.

Alan was by her side a moment later. He knelt; she could tell from the rustling of fabric and creak of the chair next to hers. Alan whispered. "We all appreciate what you're doing, taking his attention off the rest of us."

"He doesn't dare harm me, at least not until he's gotten his use out of me."

"Harm you?" Alan scoffed. "Look at you."

Abby pawed around until she was able to pat Alan's cheek. "Looking isn't my strong suit at the moment." With a grunt of pain, she turned her sightless eyes to face him. "When I'm gone, I'm counting on you to take over occupying him."

"You think he's going to release you to get medical attention?"

"No. I'm probably going to die in this third-rate theater that can't even adapt *The First Girl on Earth* properly."

"Don't say that!" he whispered harshly. She imagined him scowling around at the other hostages to make sure none of them overheard.

Abby scoffed. "I saw it on recording. Miscast Eve badly. It's objectively a bad play they put on."

"You know what I mean. You're not dying in here."

"It's an artist's duty to speak the truth, uncomfortable truths most of all. I'll hold out as long as I can, but things are grinding and gnashing that shouldn't be, and I've got old organs pulling extra duty they're not used to. The physical strain is, frankly, exhausting. How *do* you young people get through a full day without cybernetics?"

"You're evading the point," Alan said. "Tell Ned you need a doctor, a mechanic, anything. I refuse to sit by and watch you die when I know there are people just outside who can save you."

Abby found Alan's cheek again with her hand. "Good boy. You go tell him that. It'll be good practice."

Alan hesitated. "You need to tell him."

"Quite a conundrum. Either you learn to deal with Ned Lund—a small, scared, stubborn man with a tiger held by the tail—or you wait until I pass on right here in the cheap seats."

"We're in the third row," Alan pointed out. "We technically have great seats."

"Sweetie, when you can't see the stage, there's no such thing as a good seat." She laughed at her own joke until a fit of coughing forced her to stop. Spikes of pain driven down her neck, back, and legs had a way of quelling mirth.

Alan kept his thoughts to himself after that. Abby knew he was nearby from the sound of his breathing. She felt around until she found his hand and gave it a squeeze.

"I'm sorry I couldn't get you out of here."

"You got Kaylee out. That's what matters."

CHAPTER FORTY-SIX

Kaylee pulled up short when they reached the door to the upload center. This wasn't a place humans were meant to see. This was the birthplace of new robots and the site cocoon for the renewal of old ones. To her surprise, Charlie7 started down the branching path toward the mixing center for newborn robotic minds.

"Shouldn't we use the upload equipment for chassis transfers?" Kaylee asked, unsure whether it was wise to question the robot who had pioneered this technology as a middle-aged man in the waning days of the First Human Era. She'd simply been unable to help herself—or think better of it in time.

Charlie7 paused. His imposing, Version 70.2 with its matte black, almost military exterior swiveled at the hips to face her, swinging Eve's gurney and the portable rig gracefully along with it. "The upload rig for new chassis is perhaps infinitesimally better suited. However, I have a longstanding accord with the head of the Mixing Committee, and he owes me a backlog of favors. I may dry up that reserve all at once, but this is a once-in-millennium occurrence."

SPARE THE MELODRAMA. KEEP MOVING.

"You're supposed to be sleeping," Charlie7 scolded mildly as he took the admonishment to heart and resumed guiding them into the nerve center of the most important factory in the universe.

Kaylee held her breath the whole way—or felt like it, at least. She'd never been inside Kanto except the skyro repair center and the depot to pick up time-share drones. There was nothing reverential about a repair shop or a rental lot for grunt labor. But this was a place where the most brilliant minds on Earth had been handcrafted by mechanical gods.

The very thought of who had started it all suddenly cast her familiarity with Charlie7 in an irreverent light.

"I don't say it often enough," Kaylee spoke softly, confident the robot would hear her. "Or ever, actually. But thank you."

"For what?" Charlie7 asked. "This isn't a favor for you."

"For everything," Kaylee said. "For Earth not being a barren brown rock stuck in orbital space between Venus and Mars, or worse, an outpost of some freakish alien species. For not giving up on life. For not creating a race of robots and forgetting about mankind. For... all of it."

"For what it's worth, you're welcome," Charlie7 said. "But again, not a favor for you." He trudged on. They were getting close to the end. "It's my main gripe with religion, frankly. Now that I've been on God's side of Genesis, I really don't feel a need for people to keep thanking me for existing. Enjoying a nice planet and not ruining it for everyone else is all I really need."

Kaylee ruminated on that. On the one hand, it was flagrantly blasphemous and offensive even though she'd never describe herself as particularly religious. But then again, what human or robot had any right to judge him? He *had* recreated them all. He'd been alone, the sole mind for light-years, and had granted free will to stray atoms he'd pulled together into forms that resembled himself.

He wasn't all knowing—though he knew more than any one person should.

He wasn't all powerful—though he seemed to enforce his will on entire planets when he set his mind to it.

Nor was he the creator of Earth despite breathing life back into it.

Charlie7 wasn't God, but if anyone were to relate to God's emotional needs, he was the closest.

"Here we are," Charlie7 announced. "Let me do the talking."

POPPYCOCK. I'LL TALK TO HIM. YOU'RE JUST A FORKLIFT RIGHT NOW.

Kaylee bit the inside of her cheek. For someone whom she'd just shown such deference and gratitude, it was jarring to hear her great-grandmother berate him and insult him at one go.

Charlie13 was sitting inside the office on the far side of the door. He wore the same Version 70.2 chassis as Charlie7 but lacked the easy manner that filed the rough edges from the imposing metal frame. The director of the mixing center was perhaps the most influential single robot in the world—at least by legitimate means. Elbows propped on his desk, the mixing master tapped the fingers of one hand against the fingers of the other.

"I've been waiting for someone to dump this problem in my lap," Charlie13 said coldly.

"I can handle the technical side," Charlie7 suggested. "You can go grab a coffee and play some solitaire."

The two robots were identical in chassis but by dress and manner could hardly have been more different. Charlie13 was economical in motion, crossing the room to examine Eve as if he'd run simulations to determine the fewest steps he'd need to reach her. Charlie7 swept his arm theatrically to welcome his compatriot to inspect his human client.

"She's far gone," Charlie13 said. "How much brain function?" A sudden chuckle escaped the stoic robot. "Fine. I'll ask you directly. Honest assessment, though. Are you up for this?"

Kaylee wished she could listen in, but her portable wasn't getting copied on the messages Eve sent.

"Good enough," Charlie13 said. "No more 'dallying.'" He turned to Charlie7 and spoke aloud. "She gets more like one of us by the year anyway."

"We need a chassis," Kaylee said, speaking up to catch their attention.

Charlie13 regarded her like a specimen under a microscope. "Believe it or not, I'm not entirely unprepared for this eventuality."

Jason90 came into the room via a side door. Kaylee recognized him from news feeds related to Earth diverting resources from Mars to Kanto at his request. The sudden flare of anger at his arrival gave way to shock when Kaylee realized what he was wheeling into the room on a dolly.

"It's me!" Kaylee exclaimed.

RAISE MY VIEW.

Kaylee rushed to her great-grandmother's side. There was a motor in the back of the gurney that would raise the occupant's upper half to a reclined position instead of laying them flat. With a whir, Eve slowly rose until she could see across the room.

WHAT'S THE MEANING OF THIS?

The chassis was one of the new style, human realistic except under close scrutiny. It was an exact replica of Eve—or Kaylee, depending on the viewer's bias. There was no sign of aging, but the chassis was fully adult. If Kaylee had to judge, the last time she looked like that had been around age twenty.

HOW LONG HAVE YOU ALL BEEN SCHEMING THIS?

"Not me," Charlie13 said, holding up his hands. Obviously, Eve had included everyone on her transmissions as Kaylee followed along on her portable.

"Or me, technically," Jason90 said. "This was meant to be Rachel's chassis."

RACHEL'S BEEN DEAD SINCE BEFORE THE LIFE-LIKE MODELS CAME OUT.

"But she developed them," Jason90 replied. "This was her pet project. She built the prototype in her own image, and I've kept it up to current standards... just in case."

IN CASE YOU ALL NEEDED A ROBOTIC EVE.

There was an air of menace in the words, even typed.

"No. In case the Human Welfare Committee ever allowed Rachel to get uploaded. She scanned herself regularly, the last one days before she passed. Rachel knew that someday the restrictions would end."

Eve typed nothing for a moment.

BRING IT CLOSER.

Jason90 wheeled the chassis over to Eve's bedside. Painstakingly, Eve raised a hand to touch the metallic flesh, colored like a healthier version of her own. Her fingers twitched. At first, Kaylee took the spasm for a seizure but then realized that her great-grandmother was typing.

SHE ALWAYS WAS THE ACTIVIST. I SUPPOSE YOU'LL HAVE TO BUILD HER ANOTHER.

"You'll do it?" Kaylee asked. She clenched her fists, holding back from crushing Eve in a hug that might end their plans tragically premature.

THERE ARE STILL LIVES TO BE SAVED. YOUR SPURIOUS ULTERIOR MOTIVES DON'T CHANGE THAT. BE AWARE THAT A RECKONING MAY COME ONCE I'M NEITHER FEEBLE NOR URGENTLY OCCUPIED ON ANOTHER PLANET.

"I'm willing to gamble," Charlie7 said.

Charlie13 cast him a sidelong look. "I doubt you've truly gambled in your life."

Charlie7 smiled. "I've just never lost."

GET ON WITH IT.

"I'm proud of you, Grammy," Kaylee said, planting a kiss on a wrinkled forehead clammy with perspiration.

She stepped aside as Jason90 rolled the Rachel-made chassis to the upload bed.

CHAPTER FORTY-SEVEN

Breath pumped in and out of ragged lungs. The sorry sacs of flesh had already given up. Eve's bladder was full and blinking an annoyed warning to her visual display, but the valve to discharge it was just going to have to live with never fulfilling its purpose. She kept her eyes open out of a weary sense of duty. Those tired lids would get their rest soon enough.

She was in no pain.

The doctors at Franklin Hospital had installed so many nerve blockers that she hardly felt anything at all. Oh, Eve could have disabled them with a simple command, but inviting in all those aches and urgent warnings of failing organs and threadbare joints didn't seem so much noble as it did masochistic.

How different will it really be? she asked herself as Charlie7 attached the silly helmet-like contraption that would capture her mind as it stood that very moment and whisked it off to the crystal she'd avoided for so many decades.

"You'll be happy to know," Jason90 said conversationally, "that Rachel planned ahead for a 5-petabyte crystal. I suspect we'll be needing the storage space for that super intellect of yours."

Eve began to twitch a message, but the effort didn't seem worth the inconvenience. Soon enough. Soon enough she'd have energy to spare, clear wits, and not a worry in the world.

What a load of claptrap.

Eve hadn't met a robot that wasn't a pile of neuroses walled off behind bricks of stoic bravery. Sure, the robots could hide their fears behind an emotionless facade, but she'd ventured into enough candid conversations over the years to know that, deep down, they were as addled as humans. They just kept quieter about it.

The scanner hummed. Eve felt a resonance in her skull. It conjured dark memories of being in Evelyn11's lab with metal probes staked through her brain like an iron maiden's victim. But the scan itself wasn't unpleasant; in fact, it nearly passed for a massage.

Quietly tapping into the Kanto computer system with codes she wasn't authorized to have, Eve kept tabs on the progress of the scan.

It was slow going. Vanity suggested that it was because the brain of a 147-year-old luminary was so complex, but she rather suspected the device was underpowered and methodical.

Idly, she wondered how many of her current thoughts were being captured. In a few minutes, would she even remember these final meanderings of her biological mind? Had those synapses already been scanned?

This was sheer insanity. All of it.

Blast that girl. This was all Abbigail's fault. She'd taken that "I'd do anything to keep you safe" reassurance too much to heart far too late in life. It was meant for an adventurous pre-emancipated girl venturing off into the oft-dangerous and untamed wilds of Earth. Eve had never meant it as an invitation to get herself held hostage.

And to drag poor Kaylee into this scheme? Oh, Eve was going to use her newfound vocal heartiness to give Abby a good tongue-lashing.

Suddenly, her internal display winked out.

DATA FEED CONNECTED.

BOOT SEQUENCE 00102014400.11044 SUCCESSFUL.

SYSTEM DIAGNOSTIC...

Digits flashed past, counting upward to 100 percent.

SYNCING INTERNAL CONNECTIONS...

Again, a count to 100 percent sped past Eve's vision against a dark void.

CONFIG = RACHEL18.27

CHECKING FOR UPDATES...

NO UPDATES FOUND.

SYSTEM UP TO DATE.

POWER LEVEL: 100%

```
NATIVE MEMORY: 1.94728562E+15 OF 4.5035996E+15
AVAILABLE
```

```
INTERNAL MEMORY: 1.1503652E+18 OF
1.1529215E+18 AVAILABLE
```

A list of servomotors and sensors all scrolled past, each checking out at 100 percent in the thinnest sliver of a second.

```
POWER LEVEL: 100%
```

```
BATTERY LEVEL: ERROR> NOT INSTALLED
```

```
TRUMAN-EFFECT REACTOR: 100%
```

Eve had heard so much squabbling over the diversion of Truman-Effect technology but had never considered relying on it for personal use.

```
ALL SYSTEMS ONLINE
```

```
TRANSFERRING TO MANUAL CONTROL
```

```
SUGGESTED READING: So_I'm_A_Robot_Now.V201
```

Eve's vision came alive. The interface was a variant of the one she'd been using most of her life. She could see with perfect clarity without the hassle of holding her eyelids open. Raising a hand to her eyes, she saw young flesh without any sign of wrinkles. Her joints actuated without protest or pain. Zooming in, of course, she could see the artifice in that false flesh, but at standard magnification the resemblance to human skin was uncanny.

"Grammy Eve?" Kaylee asked in a tremulous voice, leaning in with a halting smile.

"Oh, don't nanny over me," Eve said. "It worked. I remember being over there just a moment ago." She hooked a thumb behind her, where her memory of the room's layout indicated her human body ought to have been.

She supposed there couldn't be two of her.

"You can shut off the breathing assist. I believe there's a sedative available in the standard medical kit attached to that gurney." Eve had certainly had the full tour of Earth's medical protocols over the past century and a half.

"You... already did all that," Charlie7 informed her.

There were no restraints holding her to the upload rig. Unplugging cables from the back of her head with Charlie13's assistance, Eve got up and made her way to the gurney.

There lay the resting body that had carried her doggedly for so many years. "Goodbye, old friend," she said, laying a hand on the body's forehead. She turned to Charlie7. "I don't remember doing it. We must have diverged, if only for a moment at the end."

Kaylee cleared her throat. "I... don't think the other version waited to find out whether it had been successful."

Eve pursed her lips. The sensation came as a background reporting of pressure sensor data, but it felt like real touch. "I don't suppose I'd have wanted to know if it failed."

"Do you... remember everything?" Kaylee asked.

"If by that you mean that I'm pressingly needed on Mars, then yes," Eve replied. "But that also means I remember the underhandedness of every step along the way from there to here. You and Abby are going to have a lot of explaining to do once I sort this out." She addressed the latter threat to Charlie7.

"Tell Grammy Abby I'm sorry she needed to come save me," Kaylee said.

Eve cupped a hand to Kaylee's cheek. She could feel the warmth of her great-granddaughter's skin. "You're the one saving her."

"I can fly us," Charlie7 offered.

"Like fun you can," Eve replied. "Remember my threat that I'd no longer be feeble? Well, that means I no longer need a chauffeur. I'll take the access code for your spacero, and I'll leave immediately."

"Good luck, Grammy Eve," Kaylee said, throwing her arms around the Rachel-made robotic chassis.

Eve's first reaction was panic. She'd grown so accustomed to a dignified degree of frailty that her first instinct was that Kaylee was going to kill her accidentally. Her second, upon finding her great-granddaughter hanging from her neck mid-bearhug, was to measure the force of her hug in return lest she bruise human ribs.

"And let me know how the reactor works out for you," Jason90 said. "Part of my deal with Rachel was to keep her chassis cutting edge. This is the first T-E Reactor released into the wild."

Eve raised an eyebrow. "Not comforting."

"Sure you don't want that chauffeur? Just in case?" Charlie7 offered.

Eve fixed the wily old scoundrel with a wry smile. She stepped up to him on her way to the door; he had the path "accidentally" blocked. "Pardon me. I have a rescue to enact."

And with that, Eve Fourteen, the first unmixed robot in a hundred years and the first born in the Second Human Era, left Kanto.

CHAPTER FORTY-EIGHT

Kaylee turned to the ancient robots surrounding her. Amongst them, Charlie7, Charlie13, and Jason90 represented over twenty-five hundred years of wisdom and experience. She felt so small beside them, so naive and insignificant. Grammy Eve had been a wellspring of human spirit trapped in a withering shell of flesh. A moment ago, the combined efforts of these three Promethean gods had unleashed that mind in a body reborn of science.

"What now?" she dared ask.

Charlie7 affected a beleaguered sigh. "Well, I already dispatched the medevac skyroamer to Franklin Hospital. Eve took my spaceroamer. Can anyone offer a lift?"

Jason90 crossed his arms and studied the upload rig that had just produced the newborn Eve. "Anyone up for a quick vacation? I have this nagging suspicion that we're about to get flooded with requests."

"Vintage racers?" Charlie13 suggested. "I have a 1963 model Corvette that's never been touched by a drone and 1,300 liters of synthetic gasoline that's not going to burn itself."

"Sure," Charlie7 replied with an indifferent shrug. "Trans-Siberian Raceway?"

"Make it the Yangtze Basin Speedway and I'm in," Jason90 replied.

Kaylee couldn't believe her ears. "You're going joyriding?"

Charlie13 cocked his head. "I put in, on average, 164 hours a week on mix-related business. I take my leisure when I see fit. You develop a sense of timing for this sort of thing over the years."

"I haven't taken a day off in eight months," Jason90 added.

Charlie7 declined comment with a shrug. He'd been officially retired since before Kaylee was born—before Eve was born, even.

"But what about the people on Mars?" Kaylee asked.

"Solarwide news feeds," Charlie13 said. "Flag an alert if you're worried you'll miss updates."

"You're welcome to come," Charlie7 added.

Kaylee blinked, dumbfounded. Now that they spoke of vacations and days off, she realized that she hadn't taken any time for herself since moving to Mars.

And yet...

"Sorry," she said. "Alan's still in danger. It wouldn't feel right."

"Well, suit yourself," Charlie7 said. "I'll pull a string or two and get you a transport back—not in a gel pod."

"Must be nice, having a robotic chassis for a trip like that."

Charlie7 snorted. "I have no clue. Last time I had a human body, only a handful of humans had ever set foot on Mars. An old lab-rat like me certainly hadn't been. Breaking the atmosphere was for square-jawed military sorts."

Would she ever be like them? Would Kaylee ever be able to casually make reference to what things were like when "back in the day" was a thousand years gone by?

"Can you find your way back to the landing zones?" Charlie7 asked as the others gathered to depart. "We won't be taking the same departure point as you."

Kaylee nodded. "I'll manage. Thank you. All of you."

All three robots turned in rough unison. "You're welcome," each answered.

As she meandered her way back to landing zone Southeast Region-5, Kaylee's portable tracked the progress of the transport coming to retrieve her. By the speeds it was taking through Earth's atmosphere, she suspected a robotic pilot. No autopilot was authorized to reach such calamitous velocity. Fast as it approached, however, Kaylee's proximity to the landing zone gave her an insurmountable head start.

The time passed in a haze. So much had gone on in so few days. It hadn't been a full week since Alan had half-woken her in the night with a furtive plan to spy on the Chain Breakers. Once up on the rooftop level of Kanto, Kaylee performed a few calisthenics, fully aware that her next few days would be a cramped flight to Mars in a spacero the size of a reclining sofa.

The spacero arrived without fanfare, setting down a few meters from her and popping the canopy as soon as the landing feet settled.

Kaylee stretched on tiptoes in her eagerness to learn the identity of her traveling companion.

"Hi, Kaylee," Dr. Toby said with a wave. That familiar, smiling face beamed down at her. "Hop in. I've got a travel kit with everything you need including your favorite cookies."

"Mom's chocolate chip recipe?" Kaylee asked, struggling to process. "Dad, what are you doing here?" She addressed her in-laws with the casual familiarity bred by a long marriage and acceptance by Alan's side of the family.

"Transport Committee is a little touchy right now about trips to Mars. They don't want lookie-loos interfering with the negotiations. You-know-who called in a few favors."

"You owed Charlie7 a favor?"

"Actually, no. He still owed me. My son... your husband... we made a good charity case for Dr. Truman to pitch to the Transport Committee. Don't just stand there. We'll have plenty of time to chat on the way."

Four days. A hard, miserable four days of increased gravity from a constant acceleration outbound and constant deceleration upon approach. Six days was far easier on the body at lower accelerations. Two weeks and the trip was considered leisurely.

"How long?" Kaylee asked as she approached the passenger side of the cockpit.

"How soon do want to see Alan?" Toby asked in reply.

"Can you manage three and a half days?"

CHAPTER FORTY-NINE

Eve's spaceroamer stabbed a hole in the void of space. Merry little warning gauges and readouts that she was aware of without seeing them told her that the human-like chassis was having no trouble with the forces plastering her to the seat. Reaching for the dashboard controls was like pushing through a wall of thick mud, but her electroactive polymer muscles didn't jitter and shake under the strain the way a human body would have reacted.

Not that a human body could have survived a force equivalent to three hundred times Earth's gravity.

Fear had chained her for so long to that old body. It was used up but too comfortable to discard, like a favorite sweater gone too threadbare to be worn in public. Evelyn11 had done that to her, made her afraid of the robotic mind. Eve had absorbed that lesson without ever being explicitly taught. She'd feared eviction from the mind she'd fought so hard to shelter from that predator's vile plans to inhabit it.

The body had died. The Eve she had always known lived on.

Somewhere couched within that revelation lay the groundwork for undoing Ned Lund's core philosophy. He wanted to cast robotkind as villains. Certainly, they had their faults. Some had a great many. Most of the worst among them had been culled. For all Eve knew, some had gotten away with even worse crimes and either ceased their predations upon humans or disguised them so well that over a hundred years of the Human Welfare Committee's vigilance had failed to expose them.

But robots weren't all bad any more than all humans were. Frankly, Eve dared say that robots were the less likely troublemakers.

Fast as the spaceroamer was, she couldn't outrun the light speed transmissions of the news feeds across the Solarwide. News of her disappearance from the hospital had stirred a furor. Seeping past the frothing noise of panicked admirers of hers, word spread about the change of her vote on the human upload ban.

"Good gracious," Eve muttered aloud, still marveling at the ease with which speech came when tired old lungs weren't required. "They're suggesting someone kidnapped me to alter my vote...

"Well, fine. Maybe they did. But I can't go letting them tear the planet apart looking form me."

Eve keyed in a transmission to all the major news feed purveyors on Earth—Mars might get word indirectly, but some minor element of surprise still struck her fancy. "To whom it may concern: My end of life plans have been thrown like dandelion fluff on the wind thanks to this business on Mars. My choices became to die and let two worlds move on without me, groping along like cave fish in a maze, or to allow myself to become a guinea pig for a process I've long resisted so I could head off to Mars to put an end to this nonsense myself. Anyone who knows my longstanding position on nonsense can well imagine how I chose.

"If anyone is of a mind to turn over rocks or break down doors looking for me, kindly find a better use for your time. I shall next be available for public gaping and ogling at the Curiosity colony on Mars."

She cut the transmission with a harrumph.

Charlie7 could fuss over her. He'd earned the right. Eve would be damned if Earth was going to turn into a publicity circus on her behalf, though. She'd return soon enough and set about cleaning up the mess with a mop and bucket. In the meantime, she had a job to do.

Mars was fast approaching. Time to call ahead.

"Curiosity colony, this is Eve Fourteen. ETA two hours, nineteen minutes, eleven seconds."

After accounting for the transition delay, the response was immediate. *"Please repeat. Confirm passenger identity. Last known location of Eve Fourteen is Franklin Hospital on Earth."*

"Check the Earth news feeds. Just have Vehicle Airlock-7 clear for the time of my arrival."

The wait was longer the second time around. *"Um, wow. That's a lot to take in. Yeah. I can have Airlock-7 ready when you get here. So... if you don't mind me asking... what's it like?"*

Eve couldn't put a name to the voice even with her memories all stored and searchable. Presumably, the tongue-tied gentleman on the other end of the transmission was a product of Martian upbringing. "I do mind. Thank you for checking before proceeding to ask anyway. Eve out."

She might be a robot now and not some balsa wood skeleton for doctors to scuttle behind like the sweeper at a horse parade, but that didn't mean her time had become a commodity subject to casual waste. Besides, that was a highly personal question and one she had yet to explore to her own satisfaction. When she felt the time right to ruminate on it with others, it would be in the company of geriatric robots or her own close friends and family, not some stranger's voice over a speaker.

Her instinct was to relax, to slouch in her seat and browse the Solarwide on topics that might educate her in preparation for her upcoming trials. But this body couldn't relax. This mind was a watch spring wound too tight, ready to leap and pounce and zip off in a billion directions at once.

So instead of relaxing, as Eve shot at cataclysmic speed through the cosmos, she indexed her new computer core.

CHAPTER FIFTY

lan sat beside Abby in the audience of the Arthur Miller Theater, dabbing at her forehead with a damp cloth. The fabric had been torn from the hem of his inconveniently well-made hostage tunic. The water had come from his lunch ration. Whether his ministrations did anything, it was hard to tell. Alan had no first aid training, and there wasn't any medical scanner around for him to use.

They'd drugged her. Whether it was the Chain Breakers' doing or some clever guesswork by the officials on the outside dosing her food, they'd gotten a sedative slipped into her system. He suspected the children doing the deliveries had intervened, reporting the severity of Abby's pain and soliciting help to ease it.

"Everything's going to be all right," Alan whispered to her, though he knew she couldn't hear him. The hand mopping his grandmother-in-law's forehead trembled.

I can't deal with Ned Lund, he told himself. *But I have to. None of the others show any sign that they'll do it.*

Alice was picking at a meal that had gone cold an hour ago. Kripesh was catatonic. Hans and Kevin played checkers with scraps of bread crust and stale potato chips for pieces, ignoring the other hostages. Dawn had her eyes closed, lips moving silently—in prayer or meditation, Alan guessed. The rest were either sleeping or pretending to.

Ned's boots beat the floor like the drums of an invading army.

"What's the meaning of this?" he demanded.

Alan looked up, checking to see whether the leader of the Chain Breakers might possibly be focusing his fury elsewhere. His hopes sank when he met Ned's glare without meaning to.

"She's out cold," Alan said. "Overwrought? Drugged? I'm no doctor."

Ned jabbed a finger at the comatose Abby, stopping just short of a bruising impact with her temple. "This... this isn't what I need right now. I got confirmation that all those Martians stuck in Earth's brainwashing camp are coming back. She's getting results. Damn me six ways if I'm going back to waiting on Earth to send someone who can deal."

"She's old," Alan replied lamely. "There's only so much she can take. I'm sure she'll wake up soon." *Soon* was a comfortably flexible term.

Ned shook her by the shoulder. Whether he was imagining it or not, Alan thought he could hear joints grinding with Abby's every limp motion.

Alan thrust Ned's hand aside. No sooner had he separated the terraformer from Abby but that hand came and slapped him across the face. "Don't you touch me!"

"You need a negotiator," Alan said, blinking to clear his vision and dabbing at the side of his face to check for blood. "Let me talk to Dana."

"You?" Ned asked with a snort. "If I wanted some carpet-bagging Martian wannabe acting as a go-between, I'd have used your wife. I need someone with authority, someone who can get those Earthbound committees off their collective asses to deliver what I asked for."

Alan couldn't take it anymore. "Maybe they'll send Charlie7," he said through his teeth.

He cringed, expecting another blow from Ned's hand.

Instead, Ned chuckled. "Let 'em try. I don't care how fast that black chassis of his is. My thumb's faster." He pulled out the bomb collar remote.

Alan's hand went instantly to his neck, as if laying a hand on the device might do the least bit to save him if it went off.

"Maybe..." Ned said. "Maybe it's time to show them that if they expect to dole out items from my list one by one, they're going to have to pick up the pace. If Abbigail Fourteen would rather nap than haggle, maybe it's time I wiped another robot."

Alan shook his head. As best he knew, the only one they'd killed had been the robot Ned wanted to frame Alan for murdering. That seemed like a lifetime ago.

"Don't," Alan said. "Please don't."

"Then wake her up," Ned ordered.

Alan patted Abby's cheek. "Abby?" he whispered. "I can't do this. I need you. *We* need you. One of the robots is going to die unless you wake up and do something."

Ned scratched at the short beard he'd grown during his time away from civilized amenities. "Maybe I'll make you pick," he mused. "Guess a number, one to five."

Alan swallowed and shook his head. "Abby," he pleaded. "Please."

"Pick one," Ned insisted. "Or I'll wipe two of them. All the same to me. Maybe one and a half, since one's a defective anyway."

Alan looked up. The question was clear in his eyes.

"Everyone knows Toby521's not right in the head," Ned said. "Maybe I'll just put him out of his misery and some other poor crate of spare circuits."

There was just no getting around that Alan had a soft spot for Toby archetypes. He'd been raised by the original Toby. Dr. Toby had been every bit the father to Alan despite there being no biological connection between them. All the Toby mixes held a shred of that father figure in them.

"You wouldn't hurt a Toby," Alan said with tears in his eyes.

"Superstitious Earthling nonsense," Ned scolded. "Nobody needs Tobies on Mars. We're not afraid to work with our hands. And don't give me the saline leaks over some robot. They're not real people. They just think they are."

A shout from up on stage turned both Ned and Alan's heads.

"Boss, we... we've got a problem!" It was Wil, and the nervous stammer wasn't like him at all.

Ned perked up. "Are they trying to force their way in?" He was already headed for the steps onto the stage. Despite the prospect of violence, Alan felt thankful to be out of the line of Ned's ire.

"No," Wil shouted back. "A new negotiator."

"Well," Ned said, pulling up short in the main aisle. A grin broke out on his face. "That's more like it. Someone who can move those good-for-nothing committee chairs, you think?"

"It's Eve Fourteen," Wil replied.

Alan watched the Chain Breaker struggle to process that name. At first, the two words struck him and refused to enter his ears. Then he blinked, perhaps trying to guess what might have been said that sounded like "Eve Fourteen" but wasn't. Then reality set in, and Ned's jaw hung open.

Wil cleared his throat. "She's actually... already in the theater."

CHAPTER FIFTY-ONE

There were times when politeness dictated a certain amount of decorum. At other times, Eve judged that showing up at someone's doorstep unexpectedly in the chassis of a robot that looked like a younger version of yourself was the way to go.

The Martian colonial officials hadn't known what to do with her. With a few items from Charlie7's spaceroamer tucked away in her Kanto-supplied gray jumpsuit, Eve marched past the cordon and told everyone to keep out of her way.

They'd obeyed.

Knocking on the door, she'd been greeted by a gruff "Who's there?" as if the idiots on the inside hadn't thought to bring perimeter security cameras.

"Eve Fourteen," she stated firmly. Somehow the robots who'd programmed this model had even accurately translated how her voice sounded to herself when she spoke. "I'm coming in to work out a deal with Edward Lund, leader of the self-proclaimed Chain Breakers."

The eyes of the man showing through the sliver of open doorway widened. "I... um, I..."

"By all means," Eve said, hooking a hand to keep the door from sliding shut. In less time than the blink of the man's eye, she'd pulled building plans for Arthur Miller Theater, looked up the closure force of this particular model of door, and cross-referenced to her own chassis specifications. If it wanted to close, she could stop it. "Tell Mr. Lund I'm here."

With an effort best described as swiping a muscular output slider to maximum, Eve wrenched the door wide. The guard at the door wasn't familiar to her, but his face was referenced in the local census data. Calvin Jackson was his name, a worker on the Mars

Terraforming Initiative. She plucked a primitive wrench from his hands. "Be careful with that. You could hurt someone."

As he disappeared into the lobby of the theater, Eve found the controls for her audio receptors and tuned them higher until she could listen in on the bickering and infighting of Ned Lund's lieutenants. It seemed there was a squabble over who was going to tell him that a robot claiming to be Eve Fourteen had showed up to meet with him.

That suited her just fine. Eve strolled the lobby, examining the posters for upcoming performances with a critical eye. It was strangely comforting just how little her vision had changed. The life-like optics worked just like her own implants—or at least the biological Eve's implants.

There would come a time when she'd have to wrestle with the existential dilemmas of all robots after a crystal upgrade. Was she still the same Eve or a copy with memories of the original? But that was for later. At the present, by the shouted conversations taking place out in the theater proper, Ned would be coming soon.

The theater doors burst open. Ned Lund blustered into the lobby with a week's bearded scruff on his face and a remote detonator in his hand. "What the hell are—good God... it's true. You're one of them."

Eve stepped forward, but Ned backpedaled just as quickly. "You have twelve humans and five robots captive. I want them released."

Holding up the remote like a cross to ward away a vampire, Ned replied, "You've got my demands."

"I do. But before I give in to a single one of them, I demand to see the robotic captives."

Without the distraction of chemical emotions, Eve could work around the fury inside her and present a calm, dignified facade. How many robots had felt this loathing in her presence without ever letting on? Were the mixes any more even-keeled than a human, or did they merely hide it better?

"So... they crammed your brain in a tin can and now you're more concerned with the robots than your own flesh and blood?" Ned demanded, drawing himself up tall as if it gave him the moral high ground.

"Do you want your list of demands filled or don't you?" Eve asked.

A sly narrowing of Ned's gaze told Eve that he was up to something. "Fine. Follow me."

Ned kept watch over his shoulder, never letting Eve out of his sight. To her mild disappointment, he didn't blunter into anything along the way. All the while, as they slipped through doors meant for theater staff and into the back area of the theater, Ned never loosened his grip on the remote.

One of Ned's underlings—Lester Smythe, she recognized from old Oxford records and officiating his emancipation—opened the door for them. A Martian-born named Gregor sat atop the back of a chair with his feet resting on the seat. In his hands, the man held a device meant for aligning magnetic fields in a Truman-Effect reactor that Earth had never delivered.

Eve appreciated the irony of using the device to threaten the lives of Earth-made robots from the factory their reactor had been diverted toward.

She was less appreciative of the line of severed robotic heads that lined the dressing room table, stainless steel craniums gleaming beneath the archway of yellow bulbs surrounding the attached mirror. By the glow in their eyes, she deduced that the tangle of cables running in and out of the skulls was enough to power the brains.

"Is that the device you intend to use if your demands aren't met?" Eve asked with a nod toward the magnetic alignment tool.

Ned gave a gesture that combined a shrug and a nod. "One for the humans. One for the robots."

"This is all unnecessary," Eve said.

"From Earth, maybe it looks that way," Ned replied. "But we can't get by out here taking handouts forever, and Earth tightens our belts every time it looks like we're going to fix this red rock and turn it blue."

"Terraforming is a decades-long process," Eve said. "A week, a month, even a year isn't going to stop progress on the planetary timeline."

"Maybe I want to enjoy it myself, not wait until I'm a shriveled old shell of a man."

Gregor heaved a sigh. "I'm a more patient man, but I'm a fair one. Earth isn't fair to Mars. It never will be so long as it controls us like a puppet on strings."

Eve shook her head. "The robots aren't out to persecute you."

"Says the traitor who joined them," Ned said, spitting at her feet. "Always knew you were too cozy with them; never figured you'd go over."

"I was afraid," Eve said. "I was born as a lab experiment. If anyone had cause to fear robots, it was me and my sisters. More of them died in that lab than survived."

Ned swallowed self-consciously.

"This brain of mine was supposed to be a new crystal for a decrepit old robot who didn't want to go through upload again, who'd do any vile, despicable deed to taste, to smell, to really feel again. She once offered to put my mind into a chassis. Did you know that?"

Both Ned and Gregor shook their heads.

"Ever since, I've harbored nightmares about that lab, about being drugged and strapped down, about having my mind treated like a pile of quantum gate operations. *You* are the reason I'm in this body," she said, aiming her perfect human-replica finger squarely at Ned.

"Me?" he asked, indicating himself with the thumb of the hand holding the remote.

"Yes. You. I was going to see my family, as best I could gather them up on short notice, and give in to the failing body that I'd been born with. But no. Someone had to take my great-granddaughter hostage. And when that didn't spur me to action, my damned daughter stabs me in the heart by throwing herself before the wheels of your juggernaut."

Ned looked puzzled. Gregor nodded sagely.

"You're saying you're only a robot because Abbigail Fourteen is out there?" Ned demanded, suddenly piecing together a stick-figure image of how Abby's intricate plot had lured her.

"And now I'm telling you, as the greatest skeptic of human upload to robotic minds, that this is the next phase of human evolution."

Gregor and Ned shared a horrified look.

"Don't you know your history?" Eve demanded. "That was the stated goal of Project Transhuman. They were never meant to weather an alien invasion. That was Charles Truman improvising. These robotic shells were the cure for cancer, the cure for age-related illness of all kinds, the cure for death itself."

"Sounds blasphemous," Gregor replied mildly.

Eve threw up her hands. "So is creating worlds, if you think about it. But if you want to go off and find what came next for our ancestors, it's your protected right as humans. Personally, I feel more alive than I have in... since I can't remember when."

Ned shook his head. "No. No, I'm not having any of this. You, get out of this theater. NOW! Gregor, give her a head to take back with her. Blank."

Eve reached into the waistband of her Kanto-made pants. Charlie7's spaceroamer had the same standard emergency supplies as his skyroamer, which Eve had ridden in 732 times—a figure that sprang to mind with fluid ease, not even having to consider it. Dating back to his days in the short-lived Human Protection Agency, that had included a non-lethal means of disabling a human.

In one smooth motion, Eve drew the tranquilizer dart pistol and fired. The first shot took Gregor in the carotid artery. The second took Ned in the shoulder. Eve had reflexes that even her teenage self would have envied, allowing her to catch both men before they fell and hurt themselves.

Gregor was limp as a blanked robot. Ned was groggy and fading fast.

As Ned slumped against the wall, Eve stood over him with both the detonator remote and the improvised EMP weapon in her hands.

"How?" Ned slurred, gazing up at her with glassy eyes.

"The EMP was real, but this remote is phony," Eve told him. "Brilliant, actually. All the robots on Earth would never figure out how to disable it remotely, so they'd either be forced to give in to your ludicrous demands or come in and kill you."

"No..."

"Yes," Eve said. With the strength in her new fingers, she cracked the casing on the remote open. Even a cursory examination of the circuitry was conclusive. "It's just a light switch. You can turn those indicators on the collar on and off. Oh, how noble you'd have looked if Charlie7 or some ambitious James number had charged in here and saved the hostages, killing you and realizing that there was never a threat to the humans at all."

But Ned was no longer listening. He slumped over. Thermal vision indicated a slightly lowered body temperature and heart rate. He and Gregor would be fine.

Pity.

Gathering up the collection of heads and their temporary power supply, Eve lugged them toward the exit. Even with her hands full, she was able to open a Social channel and summon tech support to the theater door. "I'm terribly sorry about all this. If I'd suspected for a moment how much I'd enjoy a robotic chassis, I'd have come straight away."

On a minimal power feed, the five transorbital crewmen mumbled various thanks and promises to make it up to her.

Last was Toby521. "Does this mean Rachel might come back too? I miss her."

"I imagine so," Eve replied somberly. There would be no reversing course now. The river of human history had been diverted down a canal long in the making and which Eve no longer had the wherewithal—or the desire—to keep dammed off.

After she handed over the heads to a Martian team of well-meaning and questionably competent young people, Eve turned and headed back into the theater. There were still the human hostages and six more of the Chain Breakers, any of whom might decide not to come along quietly now that the game was up.

Eve had a daughter to scold and a great-grandson-in-law to safely secure for Kaylee.

As she strode confidently through the lobby, Eve reloaded Charlie7's tranquilizer gun.

CHAPTER FIFTY-TWO

Two weeks later, a crowd gathered deep within Kanto. There hadn't been a gathering like it since the mass awakening of the Project Transhuman team. Robots from across Earth and humans from both Earth and Mars were present as the upload rig thrummed.

Kaylee squeezed Eve's hand. Thanks to the miracle of modern robotics, Eve could feel the warmth of that grip, sense the hope and trepidation mixed within her great-granddaughter. On the far side of the girl—though at forty-six, Eve ought to stop thinking of her that way—was Wendy, grasping Kaylee's other hand.

Around the room, committee heads and robotic luminaries mingled with Eve's living family members, human committee members, and visiting officials from Mars. No one wanted to be left out of the moment.

The upload rig finished. A green indicator light on the side signaled a successful transfer.

Yet another identical robot stood up and wobbled, looked around the room, and swore. "Operation didn't work?" Abby asked.

Eve felt it was her duty to break the news. "Too much internal trauma."

Abby's shoulders rose and fell in a fake sigh. "Well, glad we pre-scanned. Hope I can still compose decent music."

"Could you before?" Rachel asked, poking her head from around the upload rig, where she'd been monitoring the transfer. Far from upset that Eve had co-opted her rainy-day chassis, she'd been overjoyed to come to life in the fresh-from-production version Jason90 had assembled on short notice.

At Eve's side, Phoebe shrugged. "I liked the song about the duck and the breadcrumbs." While all the base chassis were identical, Phoebe had taken no time in customizing hers with a vivid green hair teased out in spikes.

"I was six!" Abby protested.

Phoebe clucked her tongue. "A career that peaked too soon."

Despite the teasing, Abby was greeted with hugs from her robotic sisters and the still-biological members of the extended family. Eve joined in, happy for her daughter, but at the same time, there was something missing from the reunion.

"What's wrong?" Phoebe asked quietly, catching Eve alone at the back of the chamber. Now that she was aware of such things, she realized that Phoebe's voice was modulated just low enough that standard audio sensitivity settings for a robot wouldn't allow anyone else in the room to hear her.

"Nothing," Eve said. "Just prone to stoicism. Easier with emotive shutoffs."

"It's not nothing," Phoebe said. "I didn't know you for over a hundred years without picking up on things you can't hide behind a slick new chassis."

Eve shrugged, watching the gathering from behind as Abby described her experience to anyone who'd listen. They were all there, every sister but one that she'd rescued from Creator's lab so long ago. Kanto's production team had bent over backward to provide them all new chassis, shutting down a number of major projects temporarily. Everyone was so happy to be reunited.

"Plato would have hated this," Phoebe said, picking up without words what was nagging at Eve's heartstrings.

"Maybe he wouldn't have," Eve replied.

"We made Olivia the offer of a scan, and she flat-out refused," Phoebe said. "If Rachel had come up with this plan before Plato's time ran out, he'd have done the same."

Her sister was right, of course. As much as Eve feared what life would be like as a robot, she'd always been secretly intrigued as well. Every cybernetic implant had been one step closer. Plato had begrudged every medically advised device that kept him going. He took too much relish in the act of living; he wouldn't have wanted to lose that tactile sensation of life—even if new chassis designs were so tantalizingly close to replicating the real thing.

Charlie7 stepped over and inserted himself in their private musings. "You two wallflowers going to witness our final upload of the day?"

Eve had let her reminiscing distract her from the next ceremony. Informal as things were on this occasion, this was an event where everyone would be looking to her for approval.

Jason90 carted in the first chassis that didn't resemble the others. It was still human-like, but it had been slated for disposal, failing a number of quality checks that its new inhabitant insisted didn't matter. She hadn't wanted to divert resources from production that could have gone to someone else.

When the door at the far side of the room opened, Gemini crept in with tentative footsteps at odds with the monstrosity of an exoskeleton that carried her.

A hush fell over the upload chamber.

Of all the remaining humans on Earth—or Mars—no other had gone to greater lengths to cheat death day by day. In no other era of human history could the thin ribbon of flesh and bone have remained alive as anything more than a bedridden invalid. Incapable of speech, of movement, of controlling more of her biological functions, all Gemini had left was her mind. The body that the exoskeleton lugged around was more of a burden than a living thing.

Gemini paused just inside the door.

Eve stepped forward. "Come in. You've played your part in this." She walked down the parted row of guests that had cleared a path for the exoskeleton to pass and extended a hand. "Time to make good on a challenge you made me long ago."

"A challenge?" Gemini asked, her voice an echo of Evelyn's prim, cultured accent, squeezed through the meat grinder of a voice modulation box.

"You once asked how you were to redeem yourself if you never got the chance. I turned you over to Ashley390 to care for the sanctuary residents on Easter Island. They represented your own sin, even if none had been your personal creation. We," Eve said, spreading her hands to encompass most of the room, "are your legacy. You might not have had the noblest intentions in creating us, but here we are. The Second Human Era began with you. You've lived over a century in exile. Today, I would like to welcome you back to the world."

As Eve towed her along the line of attendees, the Eve series clones, newly robotic and organic alike, each offered their forgiveness in turn.

Even Charlie7, sly old cynic that he was, stood at the end of the line and clapped a hand on the exoskeleton's shoulder. "You've created some of the best friends I've ever had. Despite everything you did along the way, I forgive you too."

Eve and Rachel maneuvered the cumbersome exoskeleton into the scanning bed. Given the extent of the exoskelton's cranial connections, the scanning apparatus was superfluous. Rachel connected the upload scanner directly. Even the fresh scan was a formality, a gift to Gemini, allowing her the memory of the event that had just taken place—they could have uploaded her from one of ten thousand of her own scans.

"I should like to have enjoyed a bit more chocolate while I could still taste," Gemini said via the box.

Rachel poked her head out from behind the controls. "Oh, don't you even start on me. Give me five years—ten tops—and I'll work out synthetic taste. I refuse to go through eternity without ice cream."

As the scan got under way, Gemini reached out and took Eve by the hand. "I've always loved you."

Eve was the only one down the line who hadn't offered reconciliation. She'd danced around it and strongly suggested it but never actually come out and said the words. She hadn't wanted to catch herself in a lie.

Looking down, she saw the tears trickle from the corners of Gemini's eyes. Eve didn't see Creator there. That misbegotten failure of Charlie7's mixing skills hearkened back to the dark days when new robots were a roll of the dice. Evelyn11 hadn't come with the capacity for empathy, for compassion. One hundred thirty-one years trapped in a human body had filled that gaping chasm in her soul. This wasn't the monster that had created and killed thirteen Eves before the rest escaped.

"I forgive you," Eve told her in a whisper, just before the scan finished and the upload began.

They were all human. They were all robots. The future spread out before them with limitless possibilities.

Thanks for reading!

You made it to the end! Maybe you're just persistent, but hopefully that means you enjoyed the book. But this is just the end of one story. If you'd like reading my books, there are always more on the way!

Perks of being an Email Insider include:

- Notification of book releases (often with discounts)
- Inside track on beta reading
- Advance review copies (ARCs)
- Access to Inside Exclusive bonus extras and giveaways
- Best of my blog about fantasy, science fiction, and the art of worldbuilding

Sign up for the my Email Insiders list at:
jsmorin.com/updates

Books by J.S. Morin

Black Ocean: Galaxy Outlaws

Black Ocean is a fast-paced fantasy space opera series about the small crew of the *Mobius* trying to squeeze out a living. If you love fantasy and sci-fi, and still lament over the cancellation of *Firefly*, *Black Ocean* is the series for you!

Read about all of the *Black Ocean: Galaxy Outlaws* missions and discover where to buy at: **galaxyoutlawsmissions.com**

Black Ocean: Astral Prime

Co-written with author M.A. Larkin, the *Black Ocean: Astral Prime* series hearkens back to location-based space sci-fi classics like *Babylon 5* and *Star Trek: Deep Space Nine*. *Astral Prime* builds on the rich *Black Ocean* universe, introducing a colorful cast of characters for new and returning readers alike. Come along for the ride as a minor outpost in the middle of nowhere becomes a key point of interstellar conflict.

Read about the *Black Ocean: Astral Prime* series and discover where to buy on J.S. Morin's site at: **astralprimemissions.com**

Black Ocean: Mercy for Hire

The galaxy's worst bounty hunter just might be its most relentless hero.

Black Ocean: Mercy for Hire follows the exploits of a pair of do-gooder bounty hunters who care more about saving the day than getting a payday. *Mercy for Hire* also builds on the rich *Black Ocean* universe with a couple of fan favorite characters from the original series and introduces a colorful cast. Fans of vigilante justice and heroes who exemplify the word will love this series.

Read about the *Black Ocean: Mercy for Hire* series and discover where to buy at:

mercyforhiremissions.com

Twinborn Chronicles: *Awakening*

Experience the journey of mundane scribe Kyrus Hinterdale who discovers what it means to be Twinborn—and the dangers of getting caught using magic in a world that thinks it exists only in children's stories.

Twinborn Chronicles: *War of 3 Worlds*

Then continue on into the world of Korr, where the Mad Tinker and his daughter try to save the humans from the oppressive race of Kuduks. When their war spills over into both Tellurak and Veydrus, what alliances will they need to forge to make sure the right side wins?

Read about the full *Twinborn Chronicles* saga and discover where to buy at: **twinbornchronicles.com**

Project Transhuman

Project Transhuman brings genetic engineering into a post-apocalyptic Earth, 1000 years aliens obliterated all life.

These days, even the humans *are built by robots.*

Charlie7 is the oldest robot alive. He's seen everything from the fall of mankind at the hands of alien invaders to the rebuilding of a living world from the algae up. But what he hasn't seen in over a thousand years is a healthy, intelligent human. When Eve stumbles into his life, the old robot finally has something worth coming out of retirement for: someone to protect.

Read about all of the *Project Transhuman* books and discover where to buy at: **projecttranshuman.com**

Sins of Angels

Co-written with author M.A. Larkin, *Sins of Angels* is an epic galactic empire dystopian series set 3000 years after the fall of Earth. With the scope of *Dune* and the adventurous spirit of *Indiana Jones*, it delivers a conflict that spans galaxies and rests on the spirit of brave researcher Professor Rachel Jordan. Follow the complete saga, and watch as the fate of our species hangs in the balance.

Read about *Sins of Angels* and discover where to buy at:
sinsofangelsbooks.com

Shadowblood Heir

Shadowblood Heir explores what would happen if the writer of your favorite epic fantasy TV show died before the show ended—and the show was responsible. If you wonder what it would be like if an epic fantasy world invaded our world, this urban fantasy story might give you that glimpse.

Read about *Shadowblood Heir* and discover where to buy at:
shadowbloodheir.com

About the Author

I am a creator of worlds and a destroyer of words. As a fantasy writer, my works range from traditional epics to futuristic fantasy with starships. I have worked as an unpaid Little League pitcher, a cashier, a student library aide, a factory grunt, a cubicle drone, and an engineer—there is some overlap in the last two.

Through it all, though, I was always a storyteller. Eventually I started writing books based on the stray stories in my head, and people kept telling me to write more of them. Now, that's all I do for a living.

I enjoy strategy, worldbuilding, and the fantasy author's privilege to make up words. I am a gamer, a joker, and a thinker of sideways thoughts. But I don't dance, can't sing, and my best artistic efforts fall short of your average notebook doodle. When you read my books, you are seeing me at my best.

My ultimate goal is to be both clever and right at the same time. I have it on good authority that I have yet to achieve it.

Connect with me online
On my blog at **jsmorin.com**
On Facebook at **facebook.com/authorjsmorin**
On Twitter at **twitter.com/authorjsmorin**

Made in United States
Troutdale, OR
08/05/2023

11763841R00127